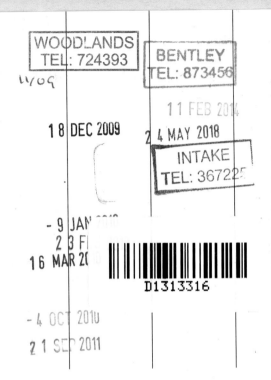

Doncaster
Metropolitan Borough Council

DONCASTER LIBRARY AND INFORMATION SERVICES

Please return/renew this item by the last date shown.
Thank you for using your library.

Available in October 2009 from Mills & Boon® Blaze®

NIGHTCAP

BY
KATHLEEN O'REILLY

MILLS & BOON

All the characters in this book have no existence outside the imagination of the author, and have no relation whatsoever to anyone bearing the same name or names. They are not even distantly inspired by any individual known or unknown to the author, and all the incidents are pure invention.

First published in Great Britain 2009
Harlequin Mills & Boon Limited,
Eton House, 18-24 Paradise Road, Richmond, Surrey TW9 1SR

© Kathleen Panov 2008

ISBN: 978 0 263 87495 2

14-1009

Harlequin Mills & Boon policy is to use papers that are natural, renewable and recyclable products and made from wood grown in sustainable forests. The logging and manufacturing processes conform to the legal environmental regulations of the country of origin.

Printed and bound in Spain
by Litografia Rosés S.A., Barcelona

Kathleen O'Reilly is an award-winning author of several romance novels, pursuing her life-long goal of sleeping late, creating a panty-hose-free work environment, and entertaining readers all over the world. She lives in New York with her husband, two children and one rabbit. She loves to hear from her readers via www.kathleenoreilly. com or by mail at PO Box 312, Nyack, NY 10960, USA.

1

CLEO HOLLINGS, DEPUTY MAYOR of New York City, glanced at her watch and groaned. Six o'clock. She needed sleep, needed sleep desperately. The city's transit strike was wearing her down, her mind manically bouncing from stalled wage negotiations to her stalled love life, and she didn't need to be thinking about her stalled love life. She needed *sleep*. Four days without it would cause anyone to get a little loopy. Only a few minutes, what would it hurt?

Gently Cleo nudged aside the massive piles of paperwork, lowering her head, her cheek nuzzling against the desk. Slowly she was lost in the sleep she so desperately desired, lost in her dreams where the impossible became possible, and the men were the stuff of legends....

THE DESERT SUN BURNED high in the sky, but here inside the great marbled walls of City Hall, she was comfortably cool. Her loyal guards waved their palm fronds and took turns offering her sips of water from diamond-encrusted goblets and feeding her the sweetest grapes on the eastern coast. Alas, her respite was soon over, and it was time for the duties that were demanded of the Empress of the East River. Majestically the trumpets' fanfare echoed as Cleo walked to the throne. As always, the needs of the city beckoned, and it was time to attend her subjects.

Her guards were ten thousand strong. Their blue transit worker uniforms a testament to their loyalty to their ruler and their city. Reverently they parted, letting her pass, and her eyes noted a newcomer's arrival with interest.

This one was worthy.

She knew it by the challenge in his mocking eyes. The man believed he could tame her—she, who ruled all of New York.

There were few men in the world that could satisfy her; however, she greeted each day with fresh optimism. When your name was Cleopatra, expectations were understandably high.

Slowly he advanced toward her throne, stalking her as effortlessly as a lion seeks prey, his bare feet making no sound in the great room. His eyes were deep-brown pools that dared her to run, but surely he knew better. Cleo never ran. Gracefully, he knelt before her with athletic ease, but he didn't lower his head in homage as men always did. Rather, his gaze never left her face, and promised her the world.

Many men had already come and tried to woo her. Their pretty words were nothing but broken promises. Their token greeting cards were trite and flowery. They plied her with the nectar from fermented grapes, but she knew those games. This…this arrogance, this *power* was new.

Cleo was intrigued.

She stood slowly, rising over him, letting him know his place in her world.

His coiled strength was unmistakable while he remained on bended knee. The hard muscles of his shoulders were tantalizingly displayed beneath the thin cloth of his toga. Strong, potent thighs supported his weight as he knelt, the tendons tight, drawing her eyes.

Her fingers stirred, eager to touch. Yet Cleo stayed immobile. This was her palace, her city, her country, and she ruled them with an iron hand that never showed weakness or mercy.

His hand reached out, as if daring to touch her, and one of her guards leaped forward, lethal spear at the ready. To touch her without invitation meant certain death, but she could not kill such a magnificent animal. Rashly, she dismissed the guards, ten thousand men who obeyed her every command. They turned to depart, their booted heels echoed in unison. As they were marching out, she admired this one's dark head, noting the silken hair and the tantalizing aroma of…Issey Miyake cologne. It was her favorite, never failing to kindle her desires.

Even while supplicated before her, his arrogant mouth inched up at the corner.

The dastardly man knew.

Once the last of the guards disappeared, the hall stood empty and they were alone. His mouth inched up even higher, yet he did not rise. Boldly, his hand slipped through the slit in her gown, and moved to her thigh, not asking for permission or approval, taking. The slight touch burned through her veins, searing her blood. His fingers were hard, rough but well schooled in the art of pleasure, stroking her like a cat, arousing a purr that rumbled through her nerves like the Seventh Avenue subway at rush hour. Cleo was pleased, relaxed and most of all, happy.

Men brought her gifts. No man brought her happiness.

For that alone, she would let him live.

"Who are you?" she asked.

"A common peasant," he answered, continuing the blissful caress, exploring her strong thighs, sliding up her leg, taking an inch higher with each tantalizing stroke.

"Why are you here?" she asked, her voice catching slightly, yet enough for him to notice, damn his impudence. His eyes darkened, and she found his impudence—tempting.

"I beg your indulgence, Excellency."

"You beg quite nicely," she offered, and he acknowledged her own impudence with a caress that was no longer flirting, but insolent indeed. Cleo swallowed, her knees weakening, and she hated that he knew her weakness, saw it, felt it inside her. Her body betrayed her, her legs parting, and as his fingers touched her, she could feel her womanly flesh swell, eager to feel his touch again. This time, the queen became his pawn.

Pawn? She would beg for no man, she was Cleopatra, ruler of all she surveyed. She would writhe for no man, she would moan for no man. Ruthlessly, she pushed his hand away. "We are done with playing. Come, before you grace me with your request. You will serve me in earnest. If you please me, perhaps you shall be rewarded."

He rose. He was a tall man, taller than she, stronger than she, but there was weakness in his eyes because of her. Cleo smiled. He thought he controlled her, he thought he ruled her. He was wrong.

No man messed with Cleo.

Insolently he pulled her into his lap, stealing her throne, setting her body on fire. "You are more than any man can resist."

"You dare," she cried, struggling to free herself, ready to call for the guards. Heedless of her protests, he turned her to straddle him and took her lips in a forceful kiss, taking what no man had taken before. Cleo fought even harder, but she could feel his hardened staff pressing against her womb and her flesh was weak, eager, waiting to be consumed.

"I dare," he whispered against her lips, impaling her on him with one fluid stroke.

Cleo gasped.

He was so large, stallion large, so thick, stretching her body, almost painfully. Surely no man could be so well-endowed. The muscles in her legs were painfully tight, but she would not give him the satisfaction he craved, the satisfaction that she craved until he was the conquered. One inch farther, and she wanted to sigh. His lids shuttered lower, nearly masking his eyes, but not hiding the need.

He took her mouth, his tongue demanding entrance. Weakly she opened her lips to him, opened her body to him, feeling his potency inside her. She had had lovers before, but none such as this, none so…virile.

As he moved within her, his hips slow and forceful, she forgot that he had usurped her throne, she forgot that he was a mere mortal in her realm. She forgot all but this blessed fullness inside her, the void that this man could fill.

There was a ruthlessness inside him, a hunger that equaled her own, and she sensed it, felt it in the steely control of his movements, his body, all that powerful strength. *All at her command.*

"What is your name?" she asked, because she had to know his name. He would be her favored one. She would appoint him to a position of power, give him a country, or a borough of his own to lord over.

"Mark," he told her.

"Mark," she whispered, and their bodies mated together, and with each powerful thrust, she knew she must keep him. He made her happy. "Mark," she whispered again. "Mark, Mark, Mark…"

AFTER TALKING HIS WAY past two security guards, and bribing another three assistants, Sean O'Sullivan stood in the office of Cleo Hollings, trying to figure out what to do now. This was the one scenario he hadn't prepared for. The Deputy Mayor of New York City was asleep at her desk and calling for some guy named Mark.

Lucky man.

The Deputy Mayor was hot. Even asleep with a ball-point pen sticking to her cheek, she was still smoking. Sean checked the clock on her desk, which read almost eight o'clock. Her office would be filling up soon, and with the transit strike in progress, all hands would be needed. This was his one shot, and it wouldn't be smart to stand here waiting to see how far this dream was going to take her. Not that he wasn't exceptionally interested.

With a regretful sigh, Sean put a hand on her shoulder and shook gently, the long, red fall of her hair spilling over his fingers. Tempting. Very, very tempting.

Her head snapped up, dark lashes opening, and she stared at Sean with amber eyes that were sleep fogged, and passion fogged still. That must have been some dream. He wanted to be in that dream.

She blinked. "Mark?"

And stone-cold reality. Sean shook his head. "No, not Mark. Sean O'Sullivan."

He smiled at her, and the passion faded from her expression, the sleep faded, and the amber eyes narrowed dangerously. "Why are you in my office? Are you here about the strike?"

This was the Deputy Mayor of administration that he had heard about. Cleo Hollings, the Wicked Witch of Murray Street. She oversaw the fire department, the police department, the transit workers that were currently giving the city fits, the speechwriters, the sanitation department and the courts. She ruled it all with an iron hand.

Cleo wasn't the best choice for what Sean needed,

but after he'd seen her picture, well, there wasn't much doubt who'd he go to after that. She had a body that men died for and the mouth that cleaved them in two. She was a challenge and Sean lived for challenges. The more impossible, the happier he was.

"I need to talk to you," he said.

"*Excuse me?* There are eight million commuters trying to get to work, and there's no buses, no subways. This is day four of the strike. Negotiations are restarting in—" she looked at the clock "—oh, no—an hour in midtown. I have to go." She made an attempt to leave, but Sean put a hand on her arm. Underneath the wool blazer, he felt the steel. A face like a china doll, a body like…*no, Sean. Not now.*

"Wait," he managed to say. "Please. I won't be long. Two minutes tops."

She stood frozen under his hand, her eyes staring at where he touched her. "You dare," she whispered.

Okay, that was just weird, but Sean was good at thinking on his feet. "Please. I'm begging here. You're pretty much my last chance."

Finally she shook her head, probably working off the last of sleep, the last of her dream. He noted the circles under her eyes. "How much sleep have you had?"

"Not enough. Tell me what you need."

"It's about a bar," he replied, regretfully removing his hand.

"*A bar?* You must be kidding. Tell me you're kidding."

All that angry fire, all that bottled passion. He could imagine what she was like in bed, a flash of red hair, her body coiled around his, arched and ready, blazing hot…. For a long, healthy moment, Sean got caught up in the idea.

"*Hello?* Bar?"

Jeez, he needed to stop. Mentally he yanked his

libido back on the leash. Sean put on his lawyer face. Much better. Almost enough to forget… "Someone in the mayor's office is messing with my brother's bar. I need to stop it." It was true. For the past two years, Gabe's bar had been cited for health violations, electrical problems, street problems and pretty much anything that a creative person could imagine. All citations without cause. Sean had fought the battles he could, but this last form letter was the bureaucratic breach heard round the world.

Sean was declaring war on City Hall.

Nearby, he could hear the rustling sounds of the office waking up. He needed to work fast. The clock was ticking. Literally. She rubbed at her neck, fingers diving into kinked muscle. Sleeping at a desk was never a good idea. He'd done it. He'd regretted it.

"You want me to fix that for you?" he asked, contemplating the smooth skin she was kneading, rashly ignoring the ticking clock. Mainly he wanted to touch her again. Her skin was fair, porcelain white, making a man imagine her without the exquisitely fitted suit.

Not now.

"What?" she asked, returning to look at him with steamy, caramel eyes that still weren't quite awake. Lust spiked straight to his cock. Sean didn't know Mark, didn't care, but right now, he hated the man. The photo in the newspaper had missed all her good parts, and Cleo Hollings had good parts in spades. The lethal strength inside her. All that emotion simmering, pressure building, waiting for the right spark to explode.

Wisely he kept that thought from his face. She knew her own appeal. Men fell all over her and she didn't tolerate it. He'd heard the stories. Some approaching mythic proportions.

"Your neck. I can rub the kink out if you want." He glanced at the clock, heard voices outside. Ignored them.

"Don't even think of touching me. What's the name of the bar?"

"Prime. There's an outline of the whole mess on your desk. It's short. I know you're busy. I need help."

"I'll check into it," she promised, then moved to leave.

Sean grabbed her arm again. Not exactly smart, but he liked feeling the current shoot through him. As a kid, he had stuck his finger in a light socket and lived to tell about it. There were certain parallels. "Why don't you let me take you out for dinner?" he asked.

With efficiency she shrugged into her coat, the black leather skimming her body, her breasts, her hips, riding down to toned thighs. "You're coming on to me, aren't you? It's not even eight o'clock, and we're running through every move in the playbook."

Well, duh. Did he look stupid? "Absolutely, I'm coming on to you. Men are very visual, simplistic creatures. Give us something to look at, and we're happy. I'd be some eunuch-man if I didn't come on to you, and I'm not a eunuch."

"No. I didn't think you were," Cleo murmured. "I'm not having dinner with you. Too busy."

It'd take more than a transit strike to keep Sean from what he wanted. "You don't eat?" he persisted.

"We've ordered in for the past four days. Deli food."

"You're disappointing me," he said, simply content to stare at her. He'd recite the entire New York State case law if he could stay here, staring, breathing. She was different, so different from anyone else. The tension crackled through her, tempting him all over again.

"Life's full of disappointments. I bet you'll survive," she told him, and yeah, he would, but if she thought he was giving up, uh, that was a big no. "Speaking of work. Need to get back to it. I'm sure you'll understand. Eight million commuters and all that…"

"I'll check in with you in a couple of days—"

She tightened her jaw, as if ready to correct him. Sean jumped in before she could.

"—of course, that's assuming you can resolve the strike in a couple of days."

It was an inflammatory comment, designed for one purpose only. To get her as worked up as he was, to see her eyes shoot flames. Not pretty, but Sean was driven by simple needs.

She quirked one brow, high and full of contempt. "Are you doubting my ability to whip ten thousand unionized transit workers into line?"

Entranced, Sean stared at her. "There was never one second of doubt in my brain that you could whip a whole army of men into line. Unionized transit workers or not."

She nearly smiled. He saw it. "Don't make me like you. I don't like people. Especially non-eunuch-men who need things from me."

He shrugged helplessly. "I have to. It's who I am."

Cleo headed for the door and he followed, down the stairs, out the building. The entire way he fought the urge to touch her. He wanted to feel that surge again. At the front gate, she paused where her driver was waiting.

"Hey," Sean called out and she turned.

"What?"

"Who's Mark?"

She tensed, those magnificent amber eyes lasering in on him. "I don't know a Mark. I don't want to know a Mark. There are no Marks. None. No. Marks. Ever."

Sean watched her leave, and then kicked up the

leaves that were littered along the pavement. He didn't care who Mark was. He'd made up his mind.

Sean was going to have her.

All he had to do was figure out how.

CLEO STARED AT HER NOTES and tried to concentrate, but as her driver maneuvered through the thick traffic, she was still feeling defensive, which was never a good thing. Especially now. Union negotiators weren't Little Bo Peeps. If they smelled blood in the water, she'd be hitting the streets tomorrow, looking for a new job, and that was an option she couldn't afford.

It was all Sean O'Sullivan's fault. She knew his type. Hot, arrogant, used to getting what he wanted. Used to wrapping women around his finger, wrapping women around other parts of him.

No, all she had to do was remember that she'd been cruising on four hours' sleep for the past four days, that the media was hammering the mayor's office, blaming her for the slow resolution (did they think the city printed money in its spare time?), that she hadn't had sex in over eight months and—no, strike that—*inappropriate.*

Her secretary called, reminded her of the press conference at noon. Cleo thanked her and hung up, focusing on the scenery of New York at a standstill. The transit workers walked the picket line outside a bus depot. Red brake lights crawled along Broadway.

It didn't help.

The idea that somebody had watched while she slept rankled her, especially because of that dream. Normally her dreams weren't that explicit. Normally when she fell into bed, there was no time for dreaming, much less anything else. Usually that didn't bother her, but today, she felt that loss in every lonely inch of her skin, her brain, her nerves.

She wanted to blame it on Mark Anthony and the Nile, but that wasn't the entire truth. No, Sean O'Sullivan was partly to blame. Mostly. Completely. With his dark eyes, that silky brown hair and the musky cologne that tickled her nose—among other places. He was a walking, talking, live-action orgasm.

The suit had been tailored. She had noticed it along with the broad shoulders and the killer thighs. Cleo had a fatal weakness for killer thighs. Helplessly she licked parched, Sahara-dry lips.

"Miss Hollings? We'll be there in ten."

"Thanks, Chris."

Her phone rang. The mayor, Bobby McNamara, i.e., her boss.

"Yeah?"

"You've talked to the transit authority negotiators, right? We can fix this?"

"Of course," she answered, shocked that he was doubting her skills. She, Cleo Hollings, who had worked one term under the current administration, one term under the previous administration and, before that, had worked her way up through the office of public housing. Cleo had earned her stripes at an early age and knew how to yell.

"I'll take care of it, boss. We're golden."

She hung up, looked out at thousands of cars trapped in bumper to bumper traffic and sighed wistfully. Union strikes did that to her. Frayed nerves or not, she needed no man.

Cleo Hollings, Wicked Witch of Murray Street, was back. No one, absolutely no one, would ever know she'd been gone.

THE LAW OFFICES OF McFadden Burnett were the largest in New York. Fourteen stories of attorneys, all in one building. It should have been a bad lawyer joke, but lawyers weren't very good at making fun of themselves. Within the walls of the 1937 art deco building worked old lawyers, new lawyers, fat lawyers, skinny lawyers, neat lawyers, schlub lawyers, men lawyers and women lawyers, but they all had one thing in common no matter their differences: the responsibility to do whatever it took to zealously defend their clients to the fullest extent of the law.

Sometimes that mandate was easy because their clients shouldn't be held liable. Sometimes not so much. As a lawyer, and as a human being, Sean O'Sullivan had learned to keep his judgments to himself.

The seventh floor was Sean's floor. Medical malpractice. Since New York was the medical capital of the world, it followed that it was also the medical malpractice capital of the world, as well. Sean didn't mind, the more the better. He loved the law. Loved the creativity of it, loved the structure of it, loved the fairness of it, as well as the unfairness of it. That was his job.

After he got into the office, he wheeled around the corner, and slid a mug of coffee onto Maureen's desk. "You got the Cannery deposition for me?"

"Digested, indexed and in the database, Sean, just like you asked." Maureen was a paralegal who had been at the firm for the last thirty-five years. With a diamond choker that must have cost a fortune, and elegant white hair that was styled at one of New York's best salons, she probably didn't need to work, but Maureen did, and Sean thanked her every day, because Maureen always knew what needed to be done and, even better, you could always count on her to deliver.

As such, Sean brought her coffee every morning and every afternoon. Two sugars. No cream, and a sprinkle of cinnamon on top. She took a sip and closed her eyes, obviously letting the caffeine rip through her veins. Then, when the ten-second break was over, she pulled out her pad and relayed the neatly stenographed messages.

"Katy called from the Environmental Fund, but the bossman heard the call come through, and he said that you're not to call her back because he wants the last of Dr. Winetrapp's affidavits completed and on his desk before lunchtime."

"Anything else?"

"He wanted to remind you about the two internal medicine docs from Mt. Sinai that you're supposed to schedule an interview for."

"Next?"

"Wilson called about the Cornell case, I asked him if this was regarding a settlement offer, he wouldn't tell me if it was regarding a settlement, but I knew it was regarding a settlement offer."

Sean nodded with satisfaction. The Cornell case was next up after his current trial was over. It was a botched surgery that if the plaintiff had a better lawyer than Wilson they'd win. A fat settlement was the way to go for Wilson, and Sean was glad the man could read the writing on the wall.

Speaking of the wall, Sean checked the clock there. Nearly eleven. His boss, Bruce, would be pulling paper clips from his teeth, but Sean didn't mind. The morning had been worth it. Getting up at the crack of dawn to watch Cleo Hollings have sex dreams, and then two hours talking to the lawyers at the hospital. Not as stimulating as Cleo, but productive nonetheless.

His brother's bar would be back in order soon. Cleo Hollings looked like she worked harder than anyone. She would fix it, although he'd have to stay on her case until she did. Not that that was going to be a problem. Staying on her case, riding her until she cracked.

Man, he had always had a thing for redheads. But redheads that barked like drill sergeants? He was still carrying the extra four inches in his shorts from when she glared at him. She had the sexiest eyes.

Maureen waved a hand in front of his face and brought his attention back to the present. "Bruce wanted to know why you're late, but I told him you called and said the transit strike was causing problems."

"I love you, Maureen. What did the Environmental Fund want?"

"You don't want to know."

He slid a hip against her desk. "I want to know, Maureen."

"Bruce will be furious. He's your boss. Fury is not a good thing for a boss."

"I want to know, Maureen."

"I can't tell you."

"You can tell me."

"I shouldn't tell you."

"You should tell me."

"Bruce will kill me."

"I won't let him. You're my favorite."

"He'll make my life miserable."

"I'll bring you Godiva every day," he bribed.

"The little mocha truffles?"

Sean nodded.

"Now, see, why can't all the lawyers be like you?"

"That's a rhetorical question, Maureen, so what did the Environmental Fund want?"

Maureen pulled her glasses from her head and read the pink message slip. "The West Side Ladies Botanical Preservation Group is trying to convert the half lot on 34th street into a park. The city has different ideas. They specifically requested you for representation, no surprise. I think Mrs. Ward who heads the society has a thing for you."

"She's nearly eighty."

"Mrs. Ward told me she has a thing for younger men," Maureen told him with a knowing glance.

Sean frowned. "I'll call Katy back." He wasn't nearly so enthusiastic anymore. Oh, well.

Maureen wagged a finger at him. "Don't forget. Little mocha truffles."

Sean tapped a finger to his brain. "Like a steel trap. No worries."

There were seventeen e-mails in his in-box. All from Bruce. All reflecting various stages of anxiety and neurosis. Everyone on the fourteenth floor called Bruce the Tin Man because he had no heart. Both literally and figuratively. Bruce was pushing sixty, had high blood pressure, high cholesterol and high anxiety, so four years ago, the talented surgeons at New York-Presby (McFadden Burnett clients) had given him an artificial heart. After the surgery, nobody at the firm could tell the difference.

"Bruuuuuuuuuuuce," called Sean, cruising into his office.

"It's about time. Why aren't you answering your cell?"

Sean pulled his phone out of his pocket. "You called? What the—?"

"Come on, O'Sullivan, where are we at?" Bruce called everyone by their last name. Apparently, calling employees by their first names indicated some semblance of humanity and a caring, giving spirit. All of Bruce's employees understood. You could only expect so much from an artificial heart.

Bruce, his face flushed and nervous, waved Sean in. The cause for Bruce's anxiety was the thirty-five-million-dollar lawsuit *Davies, Mutual Insurance v. New York General,* the individual doctors and their dogs and cats.

The hospital was part of America's third largest hospital chain, and one of McFadden Burnett's ka-ching-iest clients. The insurance company hadn't wanted to pay for a kidney transplant, saying that dialysis was all that was necessary for the patient. After the patient didn't recover, the insurance company was siding with the patient's estate, blaming the hospital for the wrong treatment that had affected the outcome. Sometimes that was truly the case, but right now, the insurance company had got caught being cheap, and they didn't like it.

That was the beauty of the legal system. One day, the bad guys were on one side, the good guys on the other, and the next, somebody had rolled the dice, messed up the board, and though the game stayed the same, the players had all traded places.

"Depositions are done. I got the medical report from the lead physician, and found a doc from Indiana who is a trial virgin, completely untouched and uncorrupted by the U.S. judicial system. He'll be perfect for court. My team's been prepping him. We're ready for trial. The insurance company is dog-meat."

Bruce took a deep breath, and popped another blood-pressure pill. "Your brother called."

"Why are you answering phones?"

"I thought it was you," said Bruce in his needy voice.

"Which brother?"

"The bar owner. He left messages for you on your phone."

Sean pulled his phone from his pocket, noted the absence of coverage and swore. He headed for his office phone and dialed Gabe's cell.

"What?"

"They shut Prime down, Sean. What the hell did you do? You were supposed to fix this problem, not make it worse. For the past two years I've been fighting with the health department, the building department, the liquor board and the gas company, but nobody's ever shut the place down before. And do you know what today is? It's Thursday and tomorrow is Friday. Do you know what people like to do on Friday? Drink."

Sean frowned. This was supposed to be fixed. "Wait, wait, wait, wait, wait. Who shut it down?"

"Some pencilhead from the mayor's office. Along with the health department. Along with the historical society. Along with the state liquor authority. It was a huge party. You should have been there."

No way. No freaking way that Cleo Hollings had done this. She was at the bargaining table. She couldn't have done it. Women didn't pull this crap on Sean. Ever.

"The mayor's office? You're sure?" he asked enunciating carefully, wanting to know exactly where the blame belonged. It would only take one short phone call from her. Thirty seconds or less. Yeah, she could have done it. And she had been mad. Tired, cranky…*frustrated.* He remembered those sleepy eyes and got himself aroused once again, which only made him madder. So Cleo Hollings really wanted to go head-to-head with him? Fine.

"Posted a notice on the door, it's all here in black and white. Not serving drinks tomorrow, Sean."

"I'll take care of it," he answered tightly. "We'll have you opened before happy hour."

"Are you sure?"

Sean's smile wasn't nice. "Nothing I can't handle."

2

STRIKE NEGOTIATIONS were stalled, and Cleo came back to her office in a foul mood. The lead negotiator had started by yelling at her, Cleo had yelled back, and things went downhill from there. When she returned to the bull pen where her offices were, Sean O'Sullivan was there waiting. He looked flushed, heated with anger and…yes, even then, resembling Mark Anthony.

This no-life stuff was starting to fry her brain.

"You had one of your little flying monkeys shut down the bar, didn't you?" he ranted, striding into her office, daring to read her the riot act—*her*—in her own office. Suddenly his hotness factor didn't matter so much, although he did have a great angry voice. Good tone, a lot of malevolence and that trace of New York that made most people fear for their lives.

Belinda, one of her interns, came and stood in the doorway. "We tried to stop him, but he knows the security guards. I'm sorry."

Cleo looked at Belinda, looked at the man. Pointed to Belinda. "I'll handle this." Belinda didn't look happy, she never looked happy, but she obeyed.

And then Cleo turned to the matter at hand. Sean O'Sullivan. "We're in the middle of a strike and I'm supposed to be running point with the transit authority. Do you honestly believe I have time to mess with you?"

"Somebody did."

"Not me," she said, defending herself because she was tired of everybody accusing her of everything. Undeservedly. Sometimes she deserved it, but not today, and especially not this.

He held up his hand, his eyes puzzled. "You didn't do this?"

"Nor did any of my little flying monkeys, either," she said, with a tight smile.

The man took a long breath and stuffed his hands in his pockets, but not before she noticed the fists. Somebody had a temper.

"Someone from this office shut the bar down."

Tony, intern number two, appeared in the doorway, and asked, "Need help, Miss Hollings? I know your meeting with the mayor is coming up. I can kick this guy out," he said, ignoring the fact that this guy could take him down in ten seconds or less. Tony was like that—loyal, yet short on brains. He'd go far in city government.

"It's a bit late for that, Tony. I'll look after it, thank you for trying." Tony gave Sean one more look and then left the office.

Cleo glanced at her watch. Tony was right about one thing, the mayor was going to be here any second, waiting for an update. "You will leave. Now is good."

The stranger slammed her door shut, and settled himself on her couch as if he planned to stay. He looked around the room, the picture of casual indulgence. "I don't care if you have time or not. Somebody in this office is screwing up my brother's life and I'm not happy about it."

"Nobody from this office is interested in your bar. I have a meeting with the mayor."

"Still haven't fixed that strike yet?" he asked, and this time, it was her hands that fisted.

Jackass. Mark Anthony? Fat chance of that. Mark Anthony would never question her governing skills, not even if he thought that Cleopatra had sabotaged his fiefdom. Okay, maybe then.

"So if there is a strike that's keeping everybody so busy," he continued, "how come someone from this office, someone from the health department, someone from the historical society and somebody from the state liquor authority are all out posting a notice on the door at my brother's bar?"

Cleo's eyes narrowed at that. Out of habit, she turned her angry voice into her soothing constituent voice. It wasn't easy, but a necessary job requirement. "I can't do this at the moment, but I promise that I'll look into it as soon as the strike is over."

"Gee, now I think I'll sleep better," he snapped back, seeing her soothing constituent voice for what is was. A sham.

"I like you better when you're nice," she ventured, which was a half truth. She liked him better when he was nice, but he got her insides all tight and humming when he wasn't. Disturbing, yet true.

"Most people do," he responded, and then pulled out a phone in the middle of her office, as if he owned the joint.

Cleo pointed at the door. The man smiled back.

Jackass.

"Mike. It's Sean O'Sullivan. How you doing? How's the wife? Really, what is this, number four? Getting busy, aren't you? So listen, talk to me here. I'm running down to the station at Prince Street, late for court, you know how it goes, and I race down the stairs, and when I get to the bottom, it's all empty, so I whap myself on the head for being such an idiot that I forgot about the strike. You guys are killing me here. You know what you're doing to my career, and don't laugh…."

Cleo watched him. Fascinated. He was a lawyer. It explained much. But who was Mike?

"I know you don't have anything to do with it, but what's the real holdup on the strike?"

"Yeah, mayor's a dickhead, I know, I know. I didn't vote for him."

Sean stood up, and began pacing around the office as he talked, completely taking over the place. He ignored her Rutgers diploma on the wall, ignored the press pictures next to it, ignored the picture of Bobby McNamara at his inauguration and even ignored the half-knitted afghan that she hadn't stitched on in ten years, but still kept her warm when absolutely necessary. He ignored everything, including Cleo.

"Pay raise of ten percent? That's nutso in this day and age, Mike. Why don't your guys take something less? I don't know. Five seems reasonable to me."

Two seemed reasonable to Cleo, but she started to pay closer attention. Mike, whoever he was, seemed to know things.

Sean nodded, stopping a moment to tap the mayor's bobblehead on her desk, which nodded back. "They're holding out for seven?"

Hell would freeze first. A seven percent raise? Was everyone in this town insane? Probably. Including her.

But she wasn't stupid. She scribbled a note and shoved it at him.

Pension?

He took it. Nodded. "Okay, so what about the pension stuff? What if the transit authority pulled a

Detroit, and put some money into a kitty, letting the unions fund it after that?"

Establishing a trust? Oh, creativity. Cunning. And it would save billions in the long run. Cleo liked that. She really, really liked that.

She scribbled a number on the paper and Sean jacked his thumb higher.

Cleo motioned her thumb down.

Sean scribbled a counter number on the paper, and Cleo pulled out her calculator and started running numbers. This could work. She looked at him with surprise. He noticed and flashed a cocky grin as if she should have never doubted him.

"I know, I know, the transit guys are whackjobs, too, but you think they'd bite? They should bite on that. I want to ride the subway again, Mike. It ticks me off. This is my city. Besides that, we're a few weeks away from Thanksgiving. You got all those kids wanting to see the parade, the giant balloons, Santa Claus. Come on, Mike, those guys can't disappoint the kids. Santa Claus uses the subway, too, and the kids know it.

"Yeah, yeah, I know. I'm a dreamer. Anyway, just wanted to put a bug in your ear. You know me, always ready to whine about something. Listen. We'll have to go out to dinner. You and Peggy and the rug rats…

"Nobody special here. Same old, same old, whoever's on speed dial is good enough for me.

"Yeah, yeah, don't think hell's freezing anytime soon…. Uh-oh, boss is yelling. Bad news. Gotta go. Thanks, Mike."

Sean hung up the phone and looked at Cleo, not missing a beat. "Can you do it?"

"I can't do it," she said, only to be contrary, because she was back to being aroused, and it ticked her off that union negotiations could affect her like that. The transit authority could fund the trust, and possibly stave off a fare hike until 2012. The mayor would be a hero.

"I bet you can do it. The city would be stupid not to put it out there. They'll save millions in the long run." He collapsed on her couch, again like he owned the place.

"Who's Mike?" she asked.

"Mike Flaherty. Legal representation for the national transit union in their civil rights cases. We went to Penn State together. And the transit authority was once a client of the firm. Not my area, but I know Mike. He's a good guy. Peg's really great." He talked like he knew everybody in New York, and she began to wonder if he did.

"Who are you?"

"Sean O'Sullivan."

"I remember your name. Who *are* you?"

"Lawyer. McFadden Burnett."

"What do you practice?" she asked, hoping he was contract negotiations. Boring, by the book, pansy-ass contract negotiations.

"Medical malpractice defense."

Medical malpractice defense? In the jungle of law, med-mal defense lawyers were the carnivores. The ones with sharp teeth and a bloodthirsty mind. Oh, it would be a sick, misanthropic woman to have that depraved factoid twist her panties in a knot. A very tight, pressurized knot. Very, very sick.

Unfortunately, all she could think about was Sean leaning over the conference room table, taking a deposition, hammering away at the witness, over and over, pounding, pounding until they were weeping for him to stop…

Very, very sick.

"You sure he can follow through?" she asked, calling upon every inch of her humanity, and methodically untwisting her panties.

Sean shrugged. "He doesn't have any reason to lie to me. Try it and see. It's a starting point for negotiations, since whatever you're doing isn't working. And don't go over five-and-a-half percent on the wage increase. Mike was saying seven, but he always shoots high by a couple of points. I played poker with him a few times. Not pretty, especially after he's had too much to drink."

"I'm going to owe you for this, aren't I?" she asked. She didn't have debts, not even a mortgage. She hated owing favors, she hated payback, but she had a feeling that Sean O'Sullivan was hard-core about payback, demanding his pound of flesh, pounding away until she was weeping….

Oh, *gawd.* This was only, *only* from lack of sleep. And possibly lack of sex, because the hallway quickie at last year's Christmas party with George from media relations did not even count in the big scheme of things. And it certainly was right up in there in Cleo's "mistakes that I won't make again" file.

Sean O'Sullivan smiled at her, with a slow show of teeth, and a look in his eyes that said, "I don't do quickies." Cleo shivered. "You'll owe me, but only if you think you can get ten thousand unionized transit workers in line in the next twenty-four hours."

She could feel the hot flash in her blood. Medical malpractice, she reminded herself, trying to stop the bubbling in her veins. It didn't help. "I can have them crying for mercy in two."

"Dinner tonight. And you're going to listen to me about Prime."

"Negotiations," she shot back.

"A drink, then," he countered. "After the talks."

She looked at him, studied that squared, stubborn jaw, considered the shadowed, take-no-prisoners gaze and scrutinized the nose that had probably been broken twice. She understood why.

"All right," she replied, against her own better judgment. She would be needed at home, and probably had only about an extra thirty minutes to herself, but that was more than enough time. In her world of transit workers, wastewater, taxation and permits, it wasn't often that a Sean O'Sullivan walked in. Nope, he was her orgasm, and she was going for it before he walked out again. "It might be late before the talks wind up," she warned.

"The later the better," he replied, tossing his card on the desk, causing the mayor's bobblehead to shake with disapproval.

In the upper cavity of her chest, there was a strange thudding, a chamber long forgotten. Sean O'Sullivan was a player, she reminded herself. A walking orgasm and nothing more. Thirty minutes and out. And hopefully, the thirty minutes would be well worth it.

Cleo took the card in her fingers, knowing it was better to get things over with, repay the favors and get back to the chaos of her own life.

BOBBY MCNAMARA, THE MAYOR OF New York City, was in his first term, a lifelong liberal, yet he had the magical ability to attract the money-backed vote of the Wall Street Republicans. The crime rate was down, unemployment was down, tax revenues were flowing like New York's finest Finger Lakes wine, and the housing bust had yet to quash the Manhattan real estate market. In the five boroughs of New York, times were definitely good. The McNamara administration had been a tremendous success, in no small part due to Cleo's long hours and hard work.

The mayor was a good-looking man, distinguished, in that fifty-year-old, news anchor way, with a gravelly voice that matched his appearance. Bobby had the usual politician's eye for the ladies, but he never stepped out of bounds, which is why he and Cleo worked together so well. There was lots of gossip over the years, but Cleo kept her nose down, Bobby kept his nose clean, and without any smoke to fuel the fire, the gossip always died away.

However, whenever Bobby was nervous, the fingers on his left hand played in the air, never staying still. Right now, Bobby seemed to be typing out *War and Peace.*

"We're getting killed, Cleo," he said, taking a moment to reread the latest headline about the strike, "STALLED," and then grimaced painfully. "Tell me you can work a miracle."

"I can work a miracle," Cleo assured.

"Really?" he asked.

"Yeah. Trust me, boss. We're fine." Okay, that was cocky, possibly stupid because she didn't know if Sean's insider info would amount to anything or not; however, he had been sure of himself. Arrogant. Confident. Attitudes like that didn't come from delusions, they were earned.

The talks were in a midtown hotel, and before Cleo left her office, she showered, changed, and yes, the green cashmere was the best date dress she kept in her office, and no, she did not pull her hair back into a ponytail because it flattered her cheekbones. It was because she needed to keep her hair out of her eyes while she ran numbers during the talks.

Happily, a mere two hours later, Cleo knew that Sean O'Sullivan had been right. The city's chief negotiator and the transit union boss were sorting out the final details of the agreement, and Cleo walked from the room, nearly dancing with the power of it.

Her first call? That was easy. A heads-up to the mayor to shave and wear the Brooks Brothers jacket in navy that matched his eyes and showed up well on television because the strike was nearly over.

City Hall was empty except for the security guards. Somehow everyone knew the strike had been settled. The security guards waved as she walked alone to her office. Cleo was dead on her feet, but there was a smile on her face. The Wicked Witch of Murray Street was smiling. Anyone who knew her would call it job satisfaction. Sean O'Sullivan would call it anticipation. He would be right.

Once in her office, she checked for new messages. If there was an emergency at home, she had to call him and cancel. The chance would be gone because Cleo didn't get chances like this often. She wanted to see him, wanted to feel his arms, his mouth. Wanted to feel those killer thighs wrapped around her, and feel her blood race. It had been so long since she felt like this, and it was selfish to want tonight. However, if they were fast, and she made it home before midnight, everything would work out fine.

There was only one message. It was from the mayor, telling her congratulations again, and asking her to set up a meeting with the Healthy New York committee first thing tomorrow morning. With the transit strike priority number one, they'd avoided the whole issue of Bobby's brainchild, a free children's clinic in Harlem and, in the mayor's words, "time was wasting."

Right.

Cleo took a deep breath and dialed.

"Yes?" Sean answered, knowing exactly who it was. Even over the phone, the sensual voice made her pulse beat faster.

"Tell me where to meet you."

"There's a place at the corner of Forty-seventh and Tenth. How long will it take you?"

Cleo peeked out the window at the streets. "Give me half an hour."

"See you then."

3

THE DRIVER DROPPED HER OFF at the address that Sean had given her, and Cleo stepped out of the Town Car.

"You need me to wait?" he asked. A congenial man, Thomas, Tommy, Stewart, Eric, something…

"No need." In a few hours the transit workers would be drifting back to work and, worst case at this time of night, she could take a cab. The November wind was kicking up and Cleo pulled her black leather coat tight. Soon she would have to move from leather to wool, but she really liked her black leather. There was probably something subliminal in that, but Cleo chose not to analyze it.

Right now, she was here to listen to Sean O'Sullivan, try to fix his problem and sneak in a six-minute orgasm as a personal aside. She had forty-five minutes before she had to be home, so time was of the essence. As a master in productivity, Cleo could get to full climax in one hundred and forty seconds. Forty-five minutes was positively utopian.

With her schedule and her life, tonight was pretty much it for the next three months, and she was pinning all her hopes on Sean O'Sullivan. Hopefully in the full forty-five minutes he would give her enough memories to get her through the winter. She smiled to herself because she suspected he would.

Gingerly Cleo stepped up to the old wooden door of the bar and then stopped, shaking her head in disbelief. The city's closure notice was nailed there prominently, and she realized exactly where he had directed her.

Prime.

She should have figured it out immediately and maybe if she was operating on more sleep, she would have.

Was it worth it to go above and beyond the call of duty, all for lust? Did she really need sex? Her womanly parts protested that it wasn't merely a rhetorical question.

Ruthlessly she ignored them, studying the fine print on the notice on the door. It was by the book, offering no clues as to who was directing this little vendetta. People thought that bureaucracy was all cut and dried, computerized and inhumane, but that was a far cry from the sordid truth. Every single employee knew the exact steps to make someone's life miserable. And that was the beauty of city government. So many opportunities for mayhem and havoc.

Not that Cleo spent her time working on petty schemes. No, she had a city that needed her 24/7. A city, and right now—a bar.

The place was definitely from another era. A green awning on the outside, a smoked glass window with old-fashioned beveling around the edges. She was admiring that beveling when Sean walked up behind her, still in the same suit that he'd been in earlier. This time, the trendy black tie had worked its way loose.

"Come on in," he invited, his eyes skimming over her, and the black leather coat wasn't enough to stop the shiver down her back. Anticipation. Ruthlessly she ignored that, too. This was business, at least for now. She stepped inside and it was as if she'd gone back in time. Three separate mahogany bars formed a U shape. The floor was oak, pockmocked from years of abuse. Even with all the imperfections it was still shiny and polished to a sparkling gleam. Pictures and even more pictures lined the wall, tacked together with tape, staples, nails and pins, and they were all pictures of people in the bar. New Yorkers over the years.

Oh, she didn't want to like this. She didn't want to like him too much. All she wanted was one orgasm, and to go back home to her nicely frantic life.

"Like it?" he asked, watching her face for clues.

Too much. "It's nice. Like a thousand bars in the city. So, tell me what's been happening." Cleo frowned, a trademarked frown that had been known far and wide to strike fear in the hearts of city workers, and sometimes even her boss.

Sean didn't even look fazed. He gestured for her to take a seat and then pulled up a stool next to her. "Two years ago, my brother Gabe bought up the space next door, and then started having some problems with the bar. Gabe, myself and my brother Daniel are on the deed, and we help out some, but it's really Gabe's bar. When it was a speakeasy back in the twenties, they called it O'Sullivans. Our great-grandfather opened the place, and over the years an O'Sullivan always ran it. It faded out and nobody really cared, and an uncle or cousin, somebody, I don't know who, split it in two, and sold off the half next door. Gabe, he wanted to get it back, to restore the place to the way it was. Anyway, the problems started when he filed the building permit. They held it up until I got a friend in the building department to give us a pass, and then after that it was a health inspection, but then I had a friend in the health department, and she helped me straighten out that mess, although it wasn't pretty. Then the pipes under the sidewalk outside needed work and they had to tear up the concrete and that lasted a month, and now we're fighting the historical building designation, and somewhere along the way, the building department took back the building permit, so we're stuck with a half-renovated bar."

He pointed to the back wall, which wasn't wood, but a canvas tarp.

Either the O'Sullivans were the unluckiest building owners in the tristate area, or else something dirty was going on—which was always a distinct possibility.

"You think this is all coming from the mayor's office?" she asked.

"It's the only place that has ties to all the agencies that have caused us problems." He sat forward, his hands pressing on his thighs and she noticed a subtle shift in him. The eyes weren't so sure anymore, not so cocky. *Family*. Nothing like family to shatter a normal person into little emotional pieces. "Can you do something?"

"Yes," she promised, and she would. This was her job; this was what she lived for. Okay, the perks were nice, but fixing the city? That was even nicer. Tomorrow, Cleo would talk to the mayor's secretary. It'd be a start.

"Then we toast," he said, pulling out a bottle of champagne from behind the counter and pouring two flutes of bubbling, fizzing champagne that hurt just to look at it. "It's my brother's best. If you don't tell him, I'll replace it before he notices it."

She lifted her glass, took the obligatory inhale, but it was him that kept drawing her senses. Champagne was for sissies.

Sean O'Sullivan was like a cauldron of steamy magic, calling her name. The intense heat warming her skin, the strong emotions tickling her nose and the taste…she couldn't imagine the taste, but her mouth was watering for a taste.

"You're being very nice about helping me out," he told her, sounding disgustingly surprised.

Cleo sighed. "I should have known you'd be a chauvinist."

The dark brows rose. "I thought I was giving you a compliment."

"If there was no surprise in your voice, it'd be a compliment. With that tone, it's a backhanded one at best. If I yell at people, if I make someone do their job, if I put huge demands on people, I'm, well…you know the word. It's not my favorite. Put a man in my shoes, with my mouth, and he'd be a hero."

"I read the article about you. Fascinating. The Wicked Witch of Murray Street. Is that why you got the nickname?"

It wasn't a story that she told often, it definitely wasn't the story she'd told the reporter, but she was tired, and she liked the way Sean's eyes focused on her with such intensity, as if she was the only woman who existed. "Right out of college, I got a job in the city's public housing office. It's a total zoo there. When I started, I was a complete greenhorn. I said please and thank-you and told people how great they were doing. Management 101. Nothing ever got done, and my performance reviews sucked eggs. Finally, after eighteen months, one of my superiors—a woman—took me aside and told me that this was New York, not Buckingham Palace, and I needed to grow a pair and that people were going to walk all over me if I kept acting nice. So I stopped, and you know what? She was right. I yelled, I got problems solved. I perfected my snarl, and people did things outside the job description for the first time in their careers. I embraced my inner dictator, and lo and behold, I got noticed. Why do you think I'm the only female Deputy Mayor on his staff?"

"I heard he likes the ladies," he remarked casually, those intense eyes focused on her mouth.

Quickly Cleo downed her champagne, feeling the buzz, but not from the alcohol. "Is that your not so subtle way of asking if I'm sleeping with him?"

"Yeah."

"No."

"I bet he's disappointed," he murmured, piercing eyes full of questions.

"I make him look good, he deals with the disappointment."

"So is there somebody?" he asked, refilling her glass.

"Is there somebody I'm sleeping with?" she clarified, wondering if that would deter him. She didn't think so. He looked like a man with one driving goal.

Her.

"Sleeping, not sleeping, dating, involved with, living with, etc. Any of the above."

"There's no one," she told him, because she didn't have space in her life for anyone.

"Good. Then who's Mark?"

Cleo felt something warm her cheeks. Some people referred to it as 'curl up and die' embarrassment. There were things she would confess, but a ludicrous sexual fantasy where she was the ruler of the world was not one of them. "He's nobody."

"You can tell me," Sean coaxed, his voice dripping with innuendo, like a man who knew she had sexual fantasies and wanted to hear them all—in explicit, step-by-step, nerve-shattering detail.

No.

"What if there is another man?" she shot back, deciding his ego was entirely too big.

He shrugged. "It's a challenge. But not impossible."

"You think you're that good?" She arched a brow in what she hoped was patent disbelief, rather than hopeful enthusiasm.

"See, that's a trap that a lot of people fall into. They think there's some silver bullet to sex. But the truth is that every woman is unique and most men are too lazy to discover that all-important fact. Every woman has that one place on her skin that aches to be touched, and it's a man's job to find it. The one way of kissing her that makes her mouth hum. That one thing that she's dying to do, but would never confess to anyone. Everything comes down to that moment when her eyes get hot and wild, and she's not seeing anyone else but you."

"And you know all that about me?" she asked, both terrified and aroused, her breath quickening with each slow and seductive word.

"Not yet," he said, and he took her right hand, turned it over, and stroked his index finger over her palm. "A woman's body is like a map. You start at one place. Then another. Then another and eventually you discover what she wants."

Cleo struggled to breathe. That sounded like a helluva lot longer than forty-five minutes.

Discreetly she sneaked a look at her watch before she remembered. She didn't have a lot longer than thirty minutes. She didn't even have a little longer. All she had was what she had, and she knew that thirty minutes was never going to cut it.

He wasn't the kind of man who did quickies, she recalled, cutting off the disappointment before it could start.

Time to leave. Time to cut her losses and scram. She kept telling herself that, but instead she sat, foolishly glued to the bar stool. Her hand was clutching his, as she fell into the dark, dangerous eyes.

"I have to leave," she said, her voice weak with what sounded like longing.

Before she could move, before she could leave, before she could come to her senses, he had pulled her into his lap. His mouth came down on hers, and longing started in earnest.

Until now, Cleo had never been a fan of kissing. When your schedule was tight, foreplay was a waste of time, but Sean O'Sullivan's kiss wasn't foreplay. This was pure, electric sex. Mouth sex.

Her wayward hands crept up his chest, not wasting the time to explore. Instead, she locked him to her, fusing one powerful male chest to her two aching female breasts. Cleo's world fell away, focusing on the feel of man-body surrounding her. A man's mouth making love to her.

This was definite longing.

Hard thighs cradled her, deliciously hard thighs, but that wasn't the best part. The best part was burning thick, throbbingly stiff against her rear, reminding her that no matter how she yelled, no matter how she swore, she was no man. At this exact moment, she'd never been happier of that fact in her life.

His hand gripped her jaw, his tongue stroking inside her mouth, so seductive, so coaxing, and she felt her mouth hum with pleasure, and her hips matched the rhythm of his tongue. Perfect, perfect rhythm. Cleo was hypnotized by the rhythm, caught up in a non-orgasmic orgasm of bliss.

A woman could get used to this bliss. A woman could turn all soft and yielding from all this bliss.

The rhythm had a sound, she could hear it in her head. One. Two. Three. Four. Five. Six. Seven. Eight. Nine. Ten. Eleven. Twelve.

The sound stopped.

The bliss stopped.

Cleo raised her head, stared at the ticking clock on the wall and swore.

She was late.

Sean was breathing fast, his eyes hot, filled with frustration.

"I have to go," she said, struggling in his grasp.

For a moment, his arm wouldn't let her go. "I'll take you out tomorrow."

"I can't."

"Mark?" he asked carelessly, and she blinked, wondering who the heck Mark was, and then she remembered and got furious at Sean because he'd made her forget. A figment of Mark Anthony was much more controllable than a living, breathing Sean O'Sullivan who made her blood steam, made her mouth hum and made her body ache for things that she didn't have time for.

Anger was so much more comfortable for her than regret and she started to snap at him until she saw the mischief in his eyes. He was going to make this difficult, and here she was really beginning to like him. "It's not that simple."

Gently his hands pushed the hair from her face, his gaze luxuriously warm, and she wanted the predator back, she needed the predator back. Sean was much easier to deal with when they were quick-tempered peers. This tempting security made her long to relax and give in, if only for a few minutes. A few hours. "It is that simple," he told her in a wonderfully soothing voice. "You say yes. I take you out for a drink. Dinner. Movie. Many options are available in Manhattan."

Cleo averted her eyes because she couldn't look at him and do this. "I'm booked up until spring."

"Was that a joke?"

"Honestly—no."

This time, her cell phone rang, reminding her that she was late.

"I have to go," she said again, not willing to commit to anything.

"Monday," he told her, pushing her out the door. "You can tell me what you've discovered about the bar."

"Maybe nothing," she answered, resisting the urge to touch her own mouth, feel the hum once again.

"Maybe something."

"I have to go," she repeated stupidly.

"I'll see you on Monday."

"What?" she asked, looking at him, puzzled.

"Go home. Sleep."

And Cleo walked two blocks south before she realized that she was headed the wrong way.

CLEO LIVED IN A TOWN HOUSE on the Upper West Side. It was one of the old stone town houses that had been built in the 1800s with the pipes from the 1800s that clanked when hot water ran through them. In the 1970s, the air-conditioning units had been added through the wall so as to not block the light. In the process, they had to knock out some of the wood trim, but when the sweltering summer came, it was worth it. The floors were the originals, extravagantly polished parquet that always smelled like lemon. Flocked wallpaper, vaguely Kennedy-esque, covered the walls and the delicate antique furniture had been in the Hollings family for four generations.

Cleo had lived here for almost her entire life.

Almost. There had been three and half years at the dorm at Rutgers and then two years after college when she'd lived with three other roommates. Life had been one long, fun party. But when she was twenty-three, that all changed, and she moved back into her mother's home.

"Mom?" she yelled, as she opened the door. Immediately she noticed the gray smoke and the burned smell in the air.

"Mom?" she asked again, feeling the panic inside her. She rushed inside and found the cause of the smells in the kitchen. A pan sat in the sink. The copper bottom burned black, steam still billowing into the room.

Cleo put a hand on the counter and calmed her breathing. Okay, not a disaster.

"Mrs. Cagle?" she called.

It wasn't Mrs. Cagle who appeared, but Elliott Macguire, Cleo's uncle, who lived on the floor below them and managed the apartments on the bottom two floors below that. "Elliott? Is Mom okay?"

"She's sleeping."

Cleo looked around and swore silently. Why was it that New York was so much easier to run than her own life? "What happened?"

"Rachel decided she wanted to cook, but she forgot."

"Where's Mrs. Cagle? She was supposed to be here. She's supposed to watch for these things. I warned her. How hard is this?" Mrs. Cagle usually covered the late afternoon and evening shift until Cleo returned from work.

"She called me after she put out the fire. I told her to go home and I'd stay with Rachel."

Cleo stared at the pan, helpless fear and anger battling inside her. Anger won. "I'm talking to the agency first thing in the morning. She's not coming back here. Mom could have been hurt. I should have been here, Elliott. This sort of thing doesn't happen when I'm here."

"You can't be here twenty-four hours a day. You've already fired four sitters, Cleo. Maybe it's time to stop and think."

No. She didn't need to think. She should have been here earlier tonight. Cleo tried to speak, but guilt clogged her throat.

"We need to talk, Cleo." Her uncle resembled his sister, a masculine, wiser version. The same blue eyes as Rachel Hollings and the red hair that had long faded to gray. He was the oldest sibling, the sensible one. Cleo shook her head.

"No. I don't need to talk, Elliott. I've barely slept for the past four days, I've been trying to get the subways and the buses and the trains moving again. I can't think very well at the moment."

Actually, most of that was true, but the last part was a flat-out lie. She could think very well at the moment. She could think too well. She knew exactly what her choices were, and she wasn't going to go there, but Elliott had a soft heart for his sister, and if she needed to take shameless advantage of it to keep up the status quo, then she'd do it, with no regrets.

His eyes looked at her sadly, and she didn't want him to look at her sadly, but again—whatever it took. However, she did raise her head and inched back her shoulders.

"Thank you. I owe you for this."

"I can't do this, Cleo. Not anymore."

She pinched two fingers against her forehead,

closing her eyes, the perfect picture of a headache. Elliott took the hint.

"She's my mother. She's your sister. We're all the family she has left. We do what we have to do."

His face said he wasn't happy, but he wasn't going to argue, and Cleo would take whatever victories she could.

"I can take over from here, Elliott. Go home and get some sleep."

"We'll talk about this later, Cleo?"

"Of course," she lied, and then closed the door behind him.

Before she took off her shoes, before she took off her watch, before she removed her makeup, she went in to check on her mother. She'd learned to do that one cold winter night a few years ago, when Cleo had come home, and immediately changed into her pajamas, only to discover that her mother wasn't in her room where she was supposed to be. Precious seconds were lost when she had to change back into clothes and shoes in order to go outside in twenty degree weather to track down her lost mother. Cleo never made that mistake again.

Her mother's room was the same way it had been when Cleo's father was alive. The double bed with the old color television set sitting on the dresser, and a picture of the three members of the Hollings family in their Christmas best (Cleo had been eight, and still had freckles—the curse of red hair and milk-white skin).

Rachel Hollings had been a beautiful woman in 1983, with the red hair that Cleo had inherited from her, and glorious blue eyes that lit up when she was happy, which she usually was around Christmas time.

Cleo stood there for a moment, watching her sleep. And then her mother's eyes opened, exposing gloriously happy blue eyes. "Margaret?"

"No, Mom. It's Cleo. I'm your daughter. Aunt Margaret is your sister." Aunt Margaret had died eight years ago, but Cleo didn't tell her mother that.

Rachel Hollings blinked, some of the happiness fading. "I could have sworn that you were Margaret. You look just like her. Are you sure you're not playing a trick on me? Margaret plays tricks on me."

Cleo sat down on her mother's bed, tucking the duvet around her. "No, Mom. Get some sleep."

"Could I have some hot tea? And maybe some cookies? Sugar cookies."

"I'm not sure that we have any."

Then Rachel Hollings mouth pursed into a tight line, and Cleo shook her head in defeat.

"Give me a little bit of time, Mom, and I'll make some for you," she said. "Do you want to watch a movie while I make them for you?"

"That would be nice. Something cheery. Maybe Doris Day or Lauren Bacall. Did you know that Lauren Bacall lives down the block from me? Nice, nice, woman, always says hello when she gets her meat from the butcher."

Cleo put on a DVD and went to the kitchen and made some cookies and tea for her mother. An hour and half later, they were done, her mother deeply engrossed in *The Philadelphia Story*.

While Katherine Hepburn was laughing it up on-screen, Cleo climbed in next to her mother and watched her drink her tea and happily munch on the sugar cookies, which Cleo had made exactly like her mother had taught her. One extra teaspoon of almond extract. The Hollings's secret sugar cookie recipe.

At the end of the day, these few moments were what counted most to Cleo. When she sat here, in the faded shadow of her mother, it felt right and warm, and she wouldn't let anyone take that away from her. Here, time was the enemy. No one could live forever. Gradually, her mother's eyes turned drowsy.

"I love you, Cleo," her mother told her, and Cleo felt her heart clutch, just like it always had from the time she was a little girl. Not many people loved Cleo, but her mother did, even when she couldn't recognize her. Cleo had always been a little too focused, a little too hard, a little too strong, but her mother's love was unconditional, even under the strain of Alzheimer's. The heart always recognized what the head refused to acknowledge.

"I love you, Mom," she told her, kissing her on the forehead. Finally, she changed into pajamas and set her alarm clock for seven. Five hours of sleep.

Five brief hours of dream-filled sleep, drifting in and out of consciousness. Cleo promised herself that when her eyes were closed and the moon was waxing low on the Hudson, they counted as dreams, uncontrollable dreams that couldn't be prevented.

She wasn't alone in her dreams. She wasn't lonely in her dreams. She wasn't even sleepy in her dreams. Wide awake, aware, waiting for him to touch her. He always watched her with dark eyes, heated dark eyes that made her wet with a look. His hands went to her shirt, flicking open the buttons there, and she wanted him to go faster, she insisted he go faster, but he put a finger against her lips, shushing her demands with soft laughter.

Such a cocky bastard, to mock her like that. He would pay, she thought, and lust stirred inside her at the idea of it.

She pulled his finger into her mouth and sucked hard. He stopped laughing, and dragged her closer, until they were chest to chest, her shirt hanging uselessly aside.

She loved the feel of his chest against hers, chest hair rubbing against her nipples, so marvelously coarse, such delightful textures. The hard steel of muscle, the smooth, sleek skin.

His mouth covered hers, starting gently but exploring and tasting, his fingers tangling in her hair, fusing her mouth to his. He tasted like champagne. He always tasted like champagne, bubbling and going to her head. Cleo slid her hands down over him, sliding over the strong ridges of his back, down lower, over his butt, so taut, so perfect for her hands.

He moaned into her mouth, his hips locked to hers, and she could feel him between her legs. So large, so marvelously large. She rocked against him, purring as she moved, because soon, very very soon… He couldn't wait long. The heavy weight that was pressing between her legs was testament to that fact.

His lips moved to her neck, over her shoulder, tempting her with a soft press, a languid lick. Cleo didn't like languid, she wanted something much more tangible. "Take me," she whispered. "Take. Me."

For a moment, he raised his head, stared, and she could feel the heat emanating from him. He was burning up with it. "You're not ready yet," he whispered, lowering his head to her breasts. Tasting her with his mouth.

His mouth pulled at the tender flesh of her nipple, sucking there. At each pull of his mouth, an answering shock of heat fired between her legs, and she wanted to feel him there, not these transitory pulses that merely fueled her desire.

Her legs slid against the flannel sheets, back and forth, but it didn't ease the ache inside her and when she heard the morning sounds of the city outside, she knew he was gone. It was a dream, unfulfilled wants conjuring up a trickster in her head. A man who teased, tormented and then disappeared before she had found her release.

So unfair.

Still, her sighs had been real. She had heard her own staggered breathing and if she tried hard, very hard, she could smell the shadow of his cologne. And in that moment, she believed.

Cleo opened her eyes, blinked against the darkness. She was alone.

Sure enough, it had been nothing more than a dream.

4

THE NEXT MORNING, the snooze alarm blared like a foghorn, and Cleo's brain felt like melted asphalt badly in need of patching. She was supposed to have slept last night. Ha. Instead she'd had dream sex that was potent enough to keep her awake until dawn. Quickly she jumped out of the cursed bed that was responsible for the cursed dreams and shook the effects of too little sleep and too much lust from her mind. She had something important to take care of. Her mother.

Ten minutes later, she was showered, seventy-five percent awake and talking to Frieda Knowlton, head of the home health agency. Cleo started the phone conversation, stating her requirements without preamble, lest there be any misunderstanding. "I don't want Mrs. Cagle back here again. I want someone new to work second shift. Someone qualified. Someone who won't let my mother set the building on fire."

"There might be some issues finding someone else to meet your standards at such short notice."

Inevitably, Cleo's foot began to tap while she put on her makeup. "It wouldn't be short notice if our home hadn't nearly burned down."

"Mrs. Cagle quickly got the fire under control," answered Mrs. Knowlton, a standard CYA maneuver.

"There was a *fire*. There shouldn't have been a *fire*."

"You have to admit, Ms. Hollings, that your requirements are extraordinarily high. We've gone through four aids in the past six months."

Cleo put the phone on speaker and pulled her brush through her hair, pulling until there was more hair on the brush than in her scalp. "It's my mother. Of course my requirements are high. Mrs. Knowlton, who is the best home health agency in the city?"

"We are."

"Do you know why I came to your agency?" she asked, wondering why she couldn't fix this. Cleo could fix anything. She could do anything. She was Deputy Mayor, but this, *this,* finding someone worthy to care for her mother? It shouldn't be impossible. There were thousands of people out there, qualified people who could do this job, but every single person had disappointed her. She'd gone through four agencies before hearing about Mrs. Knowlton's. Now, even Mrs. Knowlton was falling disastrously short.

"You came to us because we're the best in the tristate area. You won't find better, more qualified help, anywhere."

That wasn't exactly true. Cleo's first choice had been rumored to be the best. Not true. Then there was the second agency. The city had given them a gold-star rating. That had been a fiasco. And so on. Cleo was tired of accepting second-rate care simply because no one was willing to make waves.

"What happened to Janie?" Cleo asked. She had loved Janie. She had bought Janie presents, coffee from Starbucks on her way home, she had taken care of Janie's problems with her younger brother's parking ticket situation. Cleo had been on time when Janie's shift was over—almost always. There was the blizzard last winter, but Cleo couldn't be held responsible for weather emergencies.

Mrs. Knowlton cleared her throat. "She requested another assignment. She didn't like your attitude."

Cleo exhaled, rubbing eyes that felt like extra-crispy sandpaper. Every day at City Hall she had to be tough. She had learned, practiced and finally excelled at ruling New York. Obviously there were some places where the New York City System of Managerial Excellence (aka heavy-handed dictatorship) didn't work so well.

Still, this shouldn't be impossible.

No, it wasn't impossible. She needed to seize the situation in hand, remain calm and take charge.

"It's my mother we're talking about here. Am I wrong to want the best for her? Can't you hire people who can stay here without causing fire damage or letting my mother wander alone in the park? Is it such a diffi-cult thing? Is it money? I'll pay more." She didn't intend to yell, but slowly her volume increased until at last— not that there was any surprise—she was yelling.

"Ms. Hollings."

"Can you answer the question?" she snapped, dragging the brush through her hair and finding another tangle. She pulled, and voila, the tangle came free, ending up ensnared on the bristles of her brush.

"Ms. Hollings," soothed Mrs. Knowlton, but Cleo didn't want to hear soothing constituent voice. She knew what soothing constituent voice meant.

"It's a simple question."

And then Mrs. Knowlton began to laugh.

Cleo stopped midtirade. People didn't laugh when she yelled. They respected her, listened to her. "I didn't know I was amusing you."

"I'm sorry, but for a second, you reminded me of me."

Cleo put down her brush. "Of you?"

"Yes, as in when I'm talking to my husband. We've been married for over forty years and the man can't work a microwave. Sometimes I get so frustrated, I can feel my heart pumping out of my chest, and I yell, and I feel so much better afterwards."

Cleo put a hand over her heart. It was fast. "Really?"

"Oh, yes. Ms. Hollings, can I offer you a suggestion, and please don't take this the wrong way."

Cleo knew what was coming, but at least Mrs. Knowlton was now trying, and Cleo gave people high marks for trying. "Go ahead."

"Right now, you have one full-time aid working until five, and then part-time help coming in until nine. If you'd let me schedule two full-time shifts, I think you'd be very pleased with the results."

Immediately Cleo shook her head. "But I don't need two full-time aids. I'm here. I *want* to spend time with my mother. I don't need someone helping me. The apartment is too small for that many people."

Cleo didn't like health-care professionals in her home. It made her feel as if her mother was an invalid and not her mother anymore.

"Then send them home when you get there. I talked with your uncle yesterday and we both think this is for the best."

The best. Cleo hated when people talked about the best. The best thing would be if Cleo had an entire lifetime left with her mother. "I can do this, Mrs. Knowlton. I can work harder. I don't need that much sleep. I can cut back on the job." As she spoke, she could hear herself talking faster and faster. Fear. That's what this was. The white-hot fear that Cleo wasn't capable at all.

"Ms. Hollings, the hard truth is that the demands from your mother are only going to increase. You should be prepared for that. It's the nature of the disease."

Cleo spoke slowly, making sure that Mrs. Knowlton understood. "This disease will not beat me. Or her. This disease will not ruin the last few years that I have with her."

"Ms. Hollings—"

"I don't want to hear this, Mrs. Knowlton."

"All right, but will you agree to the additional help? Truly, your life will be better. You'll have some time to yourself. You need time to yourself. The stress is starting to take its toll."

"I don't need my life to be better. I don't need time to myself. My life is fine exactly the way it is."

"Will you agree?" Mrs. Knowlton persisted.

"Fine. But I don't like it."

"I know," Mrs. Knowlton said, not using soothing constituent voice, but another voice instead. A sad voice. "None of us do."

SLOWLY CLEO WORKED HER WAY through the morning's agenda, catching up on her phone calls, and spending thirty minutes arguing with Sam in public housing because that used to be her stomping ground, and there wasn't anybody that was going to feed her a line about why they needed to eliminate the low-rent subsidies.

Her next phone call was for Sean, to find out about the health inspection that his bar had supposedly failed. At first, Lucy was confused. "We didn't shut down a bar this week."

"Yes. Yes, you did. Prime. I saw the notice from the health department. It's on the door."

"Prime? Isn't that Sean's bar?"

"You know Sean O'Sullivan?" asked Cleo, wondering exactly how many women there were in the city who knew the man on a first-name basis. She looked at the crossword puzzle on her desk.

And the six-letter word for endless was A-N-A-N-T-A.

Lucy's voice was full of giddy, mindless love. "I know Sean. Everybody knows Sean. Marjorie went out with him a few times when the bar was having problems a year ago, but he told her that he wasn't good enough for her, and that she needed to find someone who was willing to treat her like the princess that she was. He said that he was a dog and wasn't worthy. Isn't that the most romantic thing you've ever heard?"

Lucy sighed into the phone, and Cleo's first inclination was to swear in a very unromantic fashion. However, Lucy probably wouldn't understand. "Ducky. What was the trouble with the bar?"

"I don't remember. Do you want me to transfer you to Marjorie? She'd know, or I can look it up."

"Do you remember if there was anything to it?"

"Any violations, you mean? No, I don't think so. The whole thing was very weird. Marjorie fixed it for him, I think."

"I bet she did," Cleo murmured to herself, not wanting to sound jealous, but sounding jealous and petty and spiteful, which was ridiculous because Cleo Hollings was Deputy Mayor of the city. She was proud of where she'd gotten and it was demeaning to be jealous of a health department secretary because she went on a few dates with Sean, who was most likely using said secretary to get what he wanted…exactly like he was using Cleo.

Cleo swore. Out loud, this time.

"What's that, Cleo?"

"Nothing."

"Hey, congrats on that strike resolution. I was hating it, hoofing thirty-seven blocks. You ever tried to walk thirty-seven blocks in heels? And Larry wanted me to wear my sneaks and carry the heels, but I told him that since I spent four hundred dollars on a pair of shoes, I was going to wear them. But he was right, not that I told him, man, that was some painful—"

"Lucy, I need to get off the phone now."

"Yeah, yeah, sure. We should get together for a coffee some time."

"I'll call you."

Lucy laughed. "Heard that one before. Call me when you need something, Cleo."

"Thanks, Lucy."

Cleo hung up, calling herself all sorts of synonyms for idiot, the six-letter *cretin* being her favorite.

For one moment she had bought into the tempting fairy tale that hot, charming, thoughtful single men like Sean O'Sullivan existed in New York City—a mythical creature as rare as the Loch Ness monster.

She didn't want to believe that Sean O'Sullivan was some mythical creature that she had created simply because she had too little sex and too little sleep. However, she had. Disappointment wasn't an emotion that she usually dwelled on, but this time, she dwelled.

A long time ago she had believed in thoughtful, charming men. A long time ago she'd been burned.

Not going to be burned again.

Sean O'Sullivan was the guy who used women to get exactly what he wanted, and right now Cleo was the person who had what he wanted. Not that she should be feeling guilty or anything. Every woman lusted after someone like him, which was why he was the perfect candidate for what *she* wanted.

A great orgasm.

That was it. It wasn't world peace, a balanced budget or a triple-A bond rating. It was an orgasm. A great orgasm.

She didn't have the time or energy for a relationship, but she missed the sex, she needed the sex, and most of all, she *deserved* the sex.

Cleo pulled out the notes on the latest sanitation facility and took the stairs to the Town Hall room, mentally preparing herself for the weekly ritual of being yelled at by a room of two hundred unhappy West Side residents. Nothing like getting yelled at to put the Loch Ness monster out of her head.

So, if that was the case, then why was she picturing him everywhere?

Probably because he was standing in the doorway of the conference room, waiting for her, smiling at her as if she was the only woman in the world.

Not going to buy into that fantasy, either.

The reason for the jump in her pulse was definitely not him. The spike in the body temp? Must be the balmy fall winds outside or the crowd in the room.

Only lust. Nothing else. Not anything more at all.

Oh, yes. Cleopatra, Queen of De Nile.

HE'D KNOWN CLEO WOULD be there. Sean made it his business to know who his opposition was—always. The fact that this time it was Cleo only made the meeting more stimulating.

The room was already packed when she took the podium, carefully not looking in his direction. Sean took a spot to the side and folded his arms across his chest, content to gaze in her direction. He was no fool.

Cleo introduced herself and immediately a hand shot

up from the front row, one of the women from the West Side Ladies Botanical Preservation Group.

"Is Cleo short for Cleopatra? I loved that movie. Elizabeth Taylor. Richard Burton as Mark Anthony."

Mark. Anthony. *Mark.* Anthony.

Last night he'd been tortured…tortured by the idea of her having another man in her life. He had convinced himself that the Mark from her dreams was his rival. Last night, he'd rolled around, beating up his sheets because Sean O'Sullivan was jealous. His brothers would have laughed at him because Sean O'Sullivan was never jealous. Ever.

Suddenly, Sean's day turned four shades happier, and Cleo turned four shades of red. Still, she refused to look in his direction, but he didn't mind. He felt too secure in his own prospects and capabilities.

"Please call me Cleo," she muttered. "Today's agenda is the proposal for the West Side sanitation facility." And for the next fifteen minutes she educated the West Side residents on why their park proposal was being sidelined in order to make room for a trash plant. Dennis Torrino, one of the other seven Deputy Mayors, was in the room, but apparently he was a coward, because Cleo seemed comfortable taking the heat.

Sean watched silently, a contented smile on his face, admiring the way she handled the unhappy crowd. This was the first time he'd seen her in action, and she was great. Tough and firm when necessary, answering questions, dodging complaints, and raising her voice at a few jokers who were giving the city a hard time. Within three minutes, she had the entire male audience entranced, possibly filled with lust as well. The female half took a little more finesse, but eventually she diffused their anger, too.

However, as she talked, she still refused to look in his direction, and he wondered what he'd done wrong. Of course, Sean spent most of his post-pubescent life talking his way out of jams with the female sex, which probably played some part in why he became a lawyer.

Sean learned early on that he was emotionally stunted, like a bull in a china shop, and women got hurt because they were fragile. A man had to be careful and Sean wasn't careful, he was reckless, so he'd fixed himself. If you laid things out right up front, and were honest, nobody got hurt.

Sean sighed, and cleared his throat. Slowly she turned her head in his direction. Finally.

"Did you have a question, sir?" It was the same voice that had been purring in his ear last night, which set off a whole brainful of memories. Sean got himself distracted, trying to remember what his question was.

Oh, right. "Surely there's a compromise in here somewhere. These people are only asking for a little space. Some flowers, some grass, a few trees in the summer." He smiled his most charming smile.

"This is Manhattan. There is no space," she replied, not swayed at all by the smile, which perturbed him.

"You're just dismissing this without any consideration at all. You haven't worked through the plans yet. You've made up your mind without knowing all the facts and the people here are being punished because of it." It was supposed to sound like an intelligent question rather than "Why are you mad at me?"

"Even if it was feasible, I don't have the budget dollars for this," she stated, answering his intelligent question with words, and responding to his subliminal question with hostile hands on her hips. Nice, curvy hips that had sat on him last night.

"Miss Hollings…" he said, probably sounding more patronizing and aroused than he should have. It wasn't a big shock that her eyes shot death rays. What was shocking was how much his cock liked it.

Her eyes narrowed and her face flushed, and the other Deputy Mayor gave her a curious look. Okay, so maybe it'd been a bad idea to let the entire room know he desired her more than…well, his life at the moment.

Her voice was icy and her eyes flashed with angry heat, telling him how cheaply she valued his life at the moment. "Do not assume that you can snap your fingers and the city will jump."

That didn't sound promising. He looked at her hard. "Excuse me?" Things had been good last night. Things had been flat-ass perfect last night, and now that he knew there was no Mark, things should be even more perfect.

She leaned against the podium, her voice crisp. "Everybody wants everything their way, but the hard truth is that everybody can't get what they want. A park would be great, but the people can't just snap their fingers and have the city think, voila, oh yeah, if the people want a park, then they deserve a park simply because the people are so…so…demanding," she finished with a flourish.

Sean worked to stay relaxed. It was difficult, but he managed. "It doesn't have to be a big park. I think the request of the people is very reasonable. We're not asking for Central Park Part II. Just some space."

"There are two separate viewpoints here, and we're not going to come to consensus today, so let's move on, shall we?"

Sean looked around, noticed the eyes of the West Side Ladies Botanical Preservation Group on him and promptly reddened. However, he did stay silent for the remainder. Not a good thing for a lawyer, even working pro bono, but he'd make it up to the group when he talked to Cleo again.

As soon as the meeting was over, he caught up with her and pulled her aside, feeling her shake at the touch of his hand. That piece of evidence cheered him even more. "What did I do? We were fine last night. Everything was good. And now this?"

She met his eyes once and then glanced away. "You looked at me in that meeting. Looked. At. Me. I felt like dinner. I didn't know what to do and I always know what to do."

She was talking fast and staccato voiced, and he was surprised to see this. Ten minutes ago, she had been calm Cleo who had manhandled two hundred upset West Side residents. Now, she was shaking like a leaf, her eyes wide, nervous…and tired.

Absently his thumb stroked her palm. Partially to soothe her, and partially because he needed to touch her. "I didn't know that you were getting this upset. You don't seem like an upset kind of girl."

"I'm not an upset kind of girl, which is why this is upsetting me. I can handle sex fine. I have no problems with sex. We're having an affair. Scratching an itch. Running for the Big O. That's all."

That's all?

She thought that was all this was?

Sean looked at her, stunned, because he'd never lost sleep over a woman before. He'd never planned his day around seeing a woman before. He'd never felt this confused about a woman before, and that from a man who knew women well. And this was after only one day. She'd caused jealousy in him after one freaking day.

That's all?

"Are you using me?" he asked, mortally offended.

Apparently that was the wrong thing to say. "Using *you?* You have a reputation, Sean. You go after the women who have what you need."

"I don't sleep with them—always," he added, because he was honest with women. Always.

"Sean…"

He dropped her hand and jammed his own in his pockets. "I like sex. I'm sorry. And I shouldn't be apologizing for this. I don't hurt people. I never make promises and I make sure that everybody ends up happy," he said defensively, even though he had no reason to sound defensive. Lawyers knew that instinctively.

"Do I look like I want to end up happy?" she said, not looking happy at all.

"Yes?"

She rubbed her eyes, and he could see the dark circles again. She needed sleep. He needed sleep now, too. And all he wanted to do was stand here in the middle of City Hall and gather her close and feel her breathe. Instinctively, he knew Cleo wouldn't approve of that, either.

"I don't know why this is bothering me so much," she said, and this time she looked at him. "I don't want it to bother me, but it does, and it bothers me that it bothers me. I'm distracted and second-guessing every decision that I make, and this is not me, and I want me back."

"Am I supposed to understand that?"

"I can't do this," she told him, and that he understood, and his gut—which underwent a peculiar, sick sensation—understood it, too. Panic. That's what that emotion was called.

"Yes, you can."

Stubbornly she shook her head. "No. I can work miracles. I can pull a rabbit from a hat, but I can't pull budget dollars from a stone." And boom, she changed the subject right out from under his feet. Back to the park project. Okay, Sean would take the hint. Not going to talk about the other night then.

"Can't we get federal funds or something? Park land has got to be on somebody's radar."

"Maybe." The calm was back in her face, now that they were off the personal subjects. Sex, she could talk about. City business, she could talk about. But anything that delved further below the surface seemed to rattle her. He'd make sure that he remembered that as well.

"See," he told her in his soothing voice.

"I said 'maybe.'" She was almost smiling. Almost smiling at him.

"In my book, 'maybe' is a yes. You have a few minutes?" He was taking a gamble, but he had about thirty minutes before the courthouse closed, and he wanted to spend twenty-nine minutes with her.

"Maybe."

"Can you get down to the old subway station below City Hall? I would love to see that place and explore."

"Maybe." This time, she was smiling. Definitely smiling at him.

5

THE OLD SUBWAY STATION was three flights of stairs below City Hall and hadn't been used in forty years, but it was kept in museum-worthy shape, brought out on special occasions, like a favorite party dress from the back of the closet. Cleo hadn't been down here in years, but today she was showing off. Showing off for Sean.

Green tiles covered the walls, and the windows on the ceiling were smoked with dirt, framed in purple amethyst and frilly black iron. Not a right angle in the place, but here she was, being impulsive and headstrong, and possibly stupid.

Cleo was passionate about everything in her life, and had always been full of strong emotions. Sean was, too. Which was a huge part of her problem. When she was with him, she felt she was clinging to the outside of the subway car, whizzing down the tracks in the dark, holding on for dear life. Part of her was scared witless, part of her was having the best time of her life and wasn't willing to let go.

Throughout the Town Hall meeting, he had confused her—twisted up her insides, made her feel lust and more. Sean O'Sullivan touched something inside her that she'd forgotten about. Until now, she hadn't known she was lonely.

For the last four years, she'd been hustling through

the custom-made world she designed, choosing to exclude the rest of it, because the rest rated many steps below her family and her job. People thought you could have all it, but you couldn't. The cost of a happy hour with friends was one less hour with her mother. Everything had a price, and most of the time it wasn't a price she wanted to pay. She had once, and he had a name: Danny DeBlasio.

She and Danny had been together for three young years, even making jokes about marriage, and everything was good until her mother started showing signs of Alzheimer's. Oh, sure, at first Danny had been fine with the situation, as would most humane people, and Danny was humane. However, when Cleo chose to move in with her mother, Danny soon realized what sacrifices were required.

Wham. Out of her life, faster than she could say, "I can't tonight." Last she heard, he married a stockbroker and they lived in a loft in the Village. She wished him well, but the experience had taught her a lesson.

A lot of people didn't value family the way that she did. A lot of people wouldn't inconvenience themselves for their own family, simply because they knew it was the right thing to do. A lot of people weren't nearly as stubbornly determined as Cleo.

Except for Sean, she reminded herself quickly.

However, that didn't change the fact that eventually, this subway ride was coming to a full stop, most likely when Cleo got the bar opened for him. So for now, hot sex was all she had.

Going down the stairs into the old station, he held her hand as if she was his best girl. He was good, she'd give him that. Cleo could usually spot a fraud a mile away.

When she was with him, she certainly felt like she was his best girl.

Nervously, Cleo lapsed into full tour-guide mode, but Sean interrupted her with a kiss.

He always interrupted her with a kiss.

Interrupted breathing, her heartbeat and, most dangerous of all, interrupted her life.

Only for a minute. What could it hurt?

They made it to the bench and she climbed into his lap as if she belonged. His mouth was so stubborn, so determined, and she melded her own stubborn, determined mouth to his. Her arms locked around his neck, her fingers tangling in the dark richness of his hair. He made her forget. Made her lose track of everything.

Cunning hands delved under her jacket, under her blouse, and she quivered just from the thought of it. This was better than Mark Anthony, better than mere dreams. This was hot skin, heavy breathing and the visceral feel of Sean O'Sullivan throbbing wickedly underneath her.

This was heaven.

He wasn't slow this time, this wasn't about seduction, his chest heaving at her wildly adventurous hand, and she nipped at his neck, oh so gently, and he shuddered in response. Now that was power. Strong, powerful, lethal, she'd never been so drawn to someone before. Heat licked around her, surrounded them, and she would have nipped again, but he had shoved aside her blouse, her bra, and his tongue was on her breast, and he nipped, not quite so gently, and she nearly screamed with the pleasure of it.

No man had ever dared before, and wantonly she rubbed herself against him, savoring his hardness, her softness. The thick edge of his sex rose, met her more than halfway, and once again, they were having sex in clothes. Sex in clothes had never been this satisfying before. Sex *without* clothes had never been this satisfying before, because he knew her. Everywhere he touched, her body shook. Everywhere he kissed, her skin burned.

A few more seconds—his mouth moved to her other breast—and she was going to come, and he hadn't even got to third base.

Now *that* was efficiency.

It was so easy to be here with him, stealing time.

"I dreamed of this," he whispered against her skin, and it was a voice she didn't know. Low, thrumming with desperate hunger, the same hunger she'd seen in his eyes earlier. It was the same greedy hunger she recognized in herself.

She pried his shirt loose, uncovering the muscled bulk of his torso. Hard, warm man-bulk that did nothing to satisfy her, only made her ache for more.

Bold fingers stole under her skirt, coming closer…

Coming closer…

Coming…

Closer…

A phone was ringing. Not hers.

Cleo and Sean swore at the same time.

"I have to go to the courthouse," he whispered in her ear, and she could feel him grinding against her, and it felt so perfect, and the ringing started all over again. "Have dinner with me, Cleo. Have pity on a man who really, *really* needs to have sex with you."

Slowly, regrettably, her sanity was restored. *Hot orgasm.* He was her hot orgasm. "Yes, I can tell," she told him with a shameless smile and a hard, slow press of her hips.

Happily, he groaned. "Don't do that. I've hurt like hell every minute of every day since I met you."

"Every day? Sean, I only met you yesterday." No wonder all the women loved him.

"Last night was a very painful night. It felt like two thousand years of celibacy."

"Really?" she asked, delighted. "How painful?"

He laughed. "That makes you happy? The rumors are true. You're a sadist."

"I had a bad night, too," she confessed, because when she was still in his lap, when his arms were still tight around her, she could confess things to him. Not everything, but it was only fair that he knew some things.

"So who was there? Me or Mark Anthony?" His eyes were warm, dark, and his gaze completely cocky.

"You figured that out?"

"In the meeting. It was the way your face matched your red hair. Wasn't a big leap. I'd be a pitiful lawyer if I missed the giveaways."

"Fantasizing about Mark Anthony is not something I usually do," she defended primly, getting to her feet, making sure her legs could still stand.

He took her in his arms, kissed her, rested his head against her forehead. "Have dinner with me. Spend the night with me. I'll make you forget all about that rat, Mark Anthony."

He didn't know how tempting it was. "I can't."

"Sometime. Anytime. This weekend?" he asked. Stubborn, determined.

"I don't think so."

"You're not going to tell me anything, are you? Give me a clue about your secret life?"

Cleo stayed silent because she liked this, liked standing here with his cologne sending tingles to her nose, and the look in his eyes sending tingles deep between her thighs.

He groaned. "I don't think I can last seventy-two hours, Cleo. I swear, I'm going to die. Men can die from sexual frustration. I've seen enough medical cases…."

Cleo rolled her eyes. "I don't think you're going to die."

"If I do, it's your fault. Lunch on Monday. We'll order in. Actually, I don't need to eat. Do you need to eat?"

"You're making me feel guilty," she said, not guilty at all. She was flirting with him. She recognized it. Liked it.

"Good. Guilt is good. You should feel guilt. Enough guilt to meet me at lunchtime on Monday?"

He wanted her to play hooky again, but during the day, when she was stealing an hour from her job. That, she could justify. As long as he didn't ask her to steal an hour from the time at home.

She nodded. "We can come down here. Nobody's around, and I have the key." It sounded forbidden and completely wicked. Cleo was on board with this plan in a big way. Sean kissed her again, long and slow.

When he lifted his head, he gave her a knowing look. "We're having an affair, aren't we? That's all, right?" he asked, throwing her words right back in her face.

Cleo, not to be outargued, had the perfect answer for him. "No. That implies sex. Until we've had sex, it's not an affair." She was splitting hairs, and as a lawyer he would know she was splitting hairs, but right now that's all she was willing to admit.

To torment her (probably), he kissed her again, and she felt the full force of a Sean O'Sullivan seduction. The world began to shake, and she realized it was the train rumbling by. Cleo sighed. "I used to like foreplay.

Now it just hurts," she said, mating their bodies together, pleased to note that foreplay tortured him as well.

The phone beeped again, and he shook his head to clear it. "Oh, darlin', I am in pain, now. Serious, serious pain." He gave her one last kiss and took off running up the stairs. "Until Monday, Cleo. And no Mark Anthony in your dreams. Only me."

With a worried frown, she watched him go.

Not a problem.

A COUPLE OF BLOCKS SOUTH of City Hall was Foley Square, the great Mecca of Manhattan justice. Sean looked around, breathing in the air of unadulterated jurisprudence, not as heady as the smell of unadulterated Cleo, but he did have a job to do, and this place was where he did his best work.

The whole block was like one giant courtroom. County, federal and state. All were represented here, and it was there that Sean felt at home. In the eyes of the courts, it didn't matter how much money you had or how well you dressed or how well connected you were. Everything was supposed to be impartial and equitable. Or at least that's what he had believed before he'd had the esquire shoved after his name. In reality, it didn't always turn out that way; sometimes the judicial system needed a little shove, and Sean had discovered that he had a talent for shoving things back into place.

The New York Supreme Court building was the place he needed to be now, and Sean climbed up the white steps, and flashed his court-issued ID to the guards. He hurried to Part 27 in time for the contested docket because he'd promised Bruce he'd walk through an agreed order on the Elias matter, a tangential litigation that had sprung up when the shit had hit the fan on the Davies case. Forty minutes and one signed order later, he went up to the judges' chambers, stopping by to say hello to Pete Wachtler—accidentally on purpose.

Pete had gone to law school with Sean, and was now clerking for the judge next door to the Honorable Judge DeGrasso, who just happened to be the Supreme Court judge presiding over Davies, and Sean had seven pending motions sitting on the judge's desk, and, with any luck, Pete would have heard how many of them were going to get quashed.

Sean knocked at the door, passed the secretary and found Pete slaving away at his desk. "It's Friday evening, and you're still here?"

"How're you doing, Sean? I was wondering how long it'd be before you showed up."

The thing about Pete, he was smart. Sean shrugged unapologetically. "See, this is why we're friends. Things are good, no complaints here."

"How's the bar treating you? The alcoholic type of hospitality bar with happy women, not the alcoholic type of legal bar with unhappy women, who also happen to be lawyers?"

"You should come in. Gabe's got a little hitch right now, we're fighting the city on something, but it should be fixed soon. All it needs is a little shove in the right direction."

"Do you guys ever think about selling the place? With all the rumors about the West Side stadium, it'd be worth a big piece of change."

Sean looked at him curiously. "I thought the stadium was dead."

"Developers are a tenacious bunch. If you take away their bone, you have to bury it really, really deep in order for them not to dig it up again. But it's just rumors.

Well, that and the problems with the Manning building on the West Side."

The Manning building was five blocks west of Prime. A huge condo development that was almost ready to start construction of what was designed to be the most expensive in Manhattan. "Problems? What problems?"

Pete shook his head. "It's a mess. You know National Bank, right, they were financing the project? Okay, they were originally Cleveland Home Mortgage, but the collapse of the subprime market around the country has killed them. They're this close to bankruptcy and trying to sell off whatever they can, including the Manning building. But with next year's Wall Street bonuses estimated to be nearly half of this year's, the superluxe, thirty-million-dollar units aren't what's hot. Surprisingly enough, it's the five-to-ten-million-dollar market that is sweet, so it's back to the drawing board, and there's a huge chunk of land waiting to be bought."

"Wow."

"See, you should think about selling."

Sean shook his head. "Gabe would have a heart attack, keel over and die before he'd give it up. You can't part a man from his dream. Where did you hear all this from?"

"Chambers talk, mainly. The judge meeting with his cronies, smoking cigars and talking real estate, as judges are wont to do when they're thinking of retirement."

"Yeah," muttered Sean, starting to think. "Politics. Everything is politics, isn't it? And speaking of, have you heard from DeGrasso's clerk how my motions are looking?"

"He told me that most of your motions were extremely creative, except for the change of venue. Spurious, my friend, and frankly, I was disappointed with you."

Sean shot Pete the finger—in the best sort of way. Pete was like Sean. He had been raised blue-collar by a dad who had been a butcher all of his life, but Pete had wanted a white-collar world—just like Sean.

Sean's dad had worked for the newspaper, one step above a butcher in the New York caste system, but not nearly enough to pay for college or new blue jeans or ski vacations at the winter break. Money had never been a thing for Gabe, he only wanted the bar. And Daniel had been smart enough to slide through school, but for Sean— Sean always wanted a little more. Pride was a nasty character flaw for a lower-class kid in New York, but that same pride made him work harder and made him fight harder still. When he wore Daniel's hand-me-downs, Sean had been miserable, so his first purchase out of law school had been a brand-new suit. Brooks Brothers, two-button closure, narrow lapels, custom all the way.

He took a hard look at Paul's Gucci jacket and laughed. "Nice suit."

"Yeah," answered Paul. "We made it, huh?"

"Yeah. You want to get a drink?"

"Nah. Going home to the wife."

"Still married? How's that working out for you?"

Pete beamed, looking genuinely happy. "It's great. Cole called. The guys from the frat are getting together for a night on the town. You in?"

Sean's mouth tightened. Most people had regrets in their life. Everyone had things they'd done that they weren't proud of. Sean didn't have many, he actually thought regrets were a huge waste of time. However, there was that *one* time when he had done something exceptionally stupid…and exceptionally cruel, and when Sean did things, he did them in a big way. And as a rule, Sean wasn't cruel—not to people who didn't deserve it, anyway.

With one exception. She had been sweet and nice, and completely undeserving of Sean, who had been a first-class bastard simply because he wanted to show off in front of his friends.

Damn.

"I don't think so."

"You're not so friendly anymore, Sean. The only reason I'm going is that I promised Sheryl that I'd do more networking. Don't you hate that word? Cole's now a VP at Chase; Jacob is running for the Pennsylvania Senate and has a thriving real estate business on the side; and Dylan is president of his own software company that's about to get bought out by somebody that I can't remember. Sheryl told me I should take advantage of my 'connections.' I told her there's nothing shameful about clerking for a judge. It's a coup. I have to go to this to make my wife happy. If I have to go, you have to go. I need the support."

Sean looked at him doubtfully. "I think I've got plans."

"It still bothers you, doesn't it? I'm glad it bothers you. You know, Marnie's not the strongest woman in the world, and sometimes I think she plays the victim too well, but you shouldn't have taken her to the party that night. A dogfight. She thought you were taking her to a frat party, and instead she wins the dog show. Congratulations, Sean." Pete shook his head.

Pete was the one who had introduced Sean to Marnie. Pete and Marnie had grown up in the same small town in South Jersey, gone to the same high school and their parents had played bridge together on Saturday nights.

"I was an ass."

"We all were, but you were more talented than most."

"Can we not talk about this?"

When Sean was a senior in college, on his way to his

dream of law school and out to impress his friends, he felt untouchable, flying above the laws of humanity and not worrying about the cost to Marnie and that piece of his soul that he'd never get back.

"So should I put you down for a 'no' on frat night?"

He looked at Pete and made up his mind. He couldn't run from that night. Better to confront it.

"Let me know when and where. And if you hear any more on the stadium rumors, tell me."

"Sure," Pete agreed with a nod.

After Sean left, he took a deep breath and felt a strong urge for conscience-easing alcohol. He was ready to go find his brothers and twist some arms, but he wanted to do one thing first.

He dialed City Hall and according to Louise, Cleo's secretary, she was in a meeting with the mayor, so she patched Sean through to her voice mail.

"It's Sean. I'm going to press for the park, because yes, trash is important, but so are trees and grass and all that other junk that people put in parks. So be prepared to lose this battle because I haven't even begun to fight, and I owe this to the West Side Ladies Botanical Preservation Group, and even more importantly, I always win.

"However, that wasn't why I called. I didn't tell you what I thought of the Town Hall meeting, and I wanted you to know. You were ripping it up with the big boys in there and I thought it was the sexiest thing I'd ever seen.

"Most women couldn't have come close to that, Cleo. I know guys that couldn't have come close, either. It's special and rare, and it's a lot of the reason that I spent last night in severe agony, which I won't go into graphic detail about because—okay, you wouldn't be shocked, which is another thing I like about you—but I think this message would go on a lot longer than it should.

"Bravo," he finished, and then stuffed his phone back in his pocket.

Cleo was tough and strong. The only woman he'd ever met that wouldn't care if he was an emotional bull in a china shop. For a second, Sean looked up the street to City Hall and grinned.

Now he had to call Gabe and convince him to have a brotherly drink.

If he couldn't have his woman, he'd have the next best thing.

Beer.

6

PRIME WAS HOSTING THE THREE O'Sullivan brothers, and yay, the renovations were finally done. Sean looked around, seeing the bar the way it should've been all along. The tarp that covered the back wall was gone. Now, the bar was surrounded by polished wooden floor and chairs, rather than right up against the wall.

"It looks really good, Gabe. Really good."

Gabe ran his hands over the smooth wood and yawned happily. "You shouldn't be that surprised. Took me all week to finish, but I did it. Do you know when our bar is supposed to open again, so that people can see the result of all my masterful handiwork?"

Sean sat at the bar next to Daniel and reached for one of the matchbooks sitting there, idly lighting a match before blowing it out. "Soon. I think. I don't know." He should have asked Cleo, but truthfully, he forgot.

Gabe looked at him sharply. "Why don't you know? You always know."

"It's Friday night. City offices are closed. I can't know until Monday."

Monday. Why not until Monday? When he'd been with Cleo, when he could see her, touch her, kiss her, he didn't worry, but now that he couldn't, the doubts started. He should have pressed her harder about the weekend. Why shouldn't she see him on the weekend?

What was wrong with that? If she had plans, she could have said that. Oh, I'm going off with friends. I have a meeting in Albany. Millions of reasons. But she'd kept completely silent.

Sean lit another match, watching the flame, letting it burn until it almost reached his skin before blowing it out.

Prudently, Gabe took the matches away. "It's Friday night. Why are you here?"

"You're my brothers. I love you guys. We don't spend enough time together." Technically they probably did, but it wasn't like in the old days. Gabe had a live-in girl-friend of two years, Tessa. Daniel, Sean's older brother, had married Catherine nearly a year ago. Yeah, they worked together at the bar on Saturdays, yeah, they played poker together once a week, but they never sat and hung out, drank beer, shot the breeze. Sean kinda missed the old days.

"I have a date with Tessa in thirty minutes," Gabe said, checking the clock on the wall. "We've seen eight movies since the bar's been closed. I haven't seen eight movies in my life before now. Please tell me you can fix this soon?"

Sean glared at Gabe and picked up another matchbook.

Daniel checked the clock as well. "Catherine has a reception, but she told me that she'd duck out by nine. She was telling me they auctioned a painting for fourteen million dollars. You'd think it'd be da Vinci or somebody you'd heard of. But it's not. *Fourteen million.* Do you know what the seller's taxes are on that kind of capital gain? I don't understand art. I can't tell her that because she loves art, and it's nice to look at, and she's really good, but why do people pay that much money for a piece of paper? Would you pay fourteen million dollars for a painting?"

Sean sighed. "Why do you think a woman can only see me during business hours?"

"She's married," said Gabe automatically.

"Maybe she's afraid of the dark. Darkophobic." Daniel had never had a lot of patience for Sean's women. Obviously this wasn't going to change now.

Gabe took the matches away from Sean again. "You're not hitting on married chicks, are you? You always said you wouldn't do that."

"She's not married," defended Sean, picking up a beer coaster and sliding it down the bar. "Married women give off vibes. You can tell." She couldn't be married. There was no way.

Gabe shook his head. "Married women do not give off vibes. She's married. Tell me why Tessa won't marry me? We've been living together for two years."

"She's not committed," muttered Sean.

Gabe glared. "Ass."

Daniel sighed. "She's committed, Gabe."

"I know she's committed."

"She is," Sean told him, because he shouldn't have teased Gabe about Tessa. "She has married woman vibes and she's not even married. That's commitment."

Daniel nodded wisely. "She's scared."

"Two years worth of scared? I could understand a few months, like Catherine."

"Yeah, Catherine married me. She knew a good thing. She jumped on it." He snapped his fingers. "I'm supposed to invite the two of you to dinner on Monday."

Sean thought for a second. "Can't go."

Daniel looked at him, confused. "No, Gabe and Tessa."

And wasn't that the best way to top off a crappy night? "What the..? Why don't I rate an invite?"

"Come on, Sean. It's a couples thing. Besides, you

said you couldn't go." Daniel still hadn't figured out why Sean was upset. This was the main reason Daniel O'Sullivan was an accountant.

"But would you have invited me if I could go? Maybe I can go."

"You'd be bored."

"What? The four of you sit around and play Parcheesi?"

Daniel grunted. "Catherine thinks it'd be good for Tessa to see happy domestication."

"Tessa doesn't need to see happy domestication. She sees happy domestication every day. We are domestically happy." Gabe poured a shot of vodka. Sean reached for it, but Gabe downed it first.

"Catherine's only trying to help. And she's got this new recipe for a flounder Rockefeller. It's not bad."

Not bad? It was a disaster. Sean looked at his two brothers, not believing they could be so clueless. "Am I the fifth wheel now? Next, the four of you are going on family vacations without me?"

Daniel looked shocked. "I haven't gone on a vacation with you since seventh grade, and I'm not about to start now. Nope. No party destinations for me. Just quiet, romantic spots. The beach house at the Hamptons was fun, though."

"I could be quiet and romantic," muttered Sean. "I could."

His phone rang and he checked the ID before sending it to voice mail. Idly, he picked up another coaster.

"Is that the married one?" asked Gabe, peering at Sean's phone.

Sean shook his head. "She's not married. I know she's not married."

"How do you know?"

"I just know."

"Forget about her," said Gabe. Sean's phone rang again. Not Cleo.

"She should have called," he told them, because she should have called. "I left a really great message on her voice mail. Why didn't she call?"

"She's married."

Sean threw the beer coaster at Gabe. Gabe stood and looked around. "The renovations do look great. All ready to open now. But, damn. Still closed."

"You'll be open soon, Gabe. I'm on it," Sean reassured him.

He picked up his jacket from the coat hook and waved. "Good thing you are, because right now I'm going to go convince Tessa to marry me."

"Good luck with that," shot Sean, only because he was pissed that it was Friday night and he was alone, and none of the women calling was the one that he wanted, and now both of his brothers were deserting him in his time of need.

Gabe stopped in the doorway, the worried look back on his face. "What am I doing wrong with Tessa?"

"Bring her flowers," suggested Sean.

Daniel shook his head. "No. Not flowers. Jewelry. Have you bought her a ring?"

Gabe looked even more worried. "I asked, but she said she's particular and I don't want to assume."

"Dude, assume," said Sean. "That's that whole 'no means yes' thing."

Daniel looked at Sean in complete understanding. "Man, I hate that. Why can't they just tell you? But no, keep it all bottled inside, and you're standing there clueless because you think one dress looks better than the other, and you tell her. Wrong answer."

Sadly, Sean stared at his older brother. "You are so boring now."

Daniel shrugged. "Hey, at least I'm not dating married chicks."

"She's not married!"

"I think she's married," argued Gabe. "Or you're loser dude. Take your pick."

"I'm not loser dude." The phone rang again. "See? Women love me. Love. Me." Sean checked the caller ID and swore. Still no Cleo.

"Then she's married," concluded Daniel, standing up, and taking his coat. They were leaving him alone. Sean hated being alone.

"Go home to your woman who's scared of commitment," he yelled, "or go play shuffleboard like boring people at Daniel and Catherine's. See if I care."

Gabe looked at Daniel and grinned. "I think he's jealous."

"No freaking way. Hell will freeze first." *She should have called.*

"Hey, since you're sitting here sulking by yourself, lock up, will you?"

"I was going to help you. Give you expert female advice. Not anymore, bro. You are on your own."

Daniel slapped Gabe on the back, and the two of them left. "Jealous. You're exactly right."

FRIDAY NIGHT AT THE Hollings household was family night because Rachel Hollings had a good day. Cleo entertained her mother and uncle with stories from work, omitting all of the naughty bits. Not that there were a lot of naughty bits, but it was enough to keep a smile on Cleo's face.

After the nightly news, Elliott left, and Cleo and her

mother worked a crossword together. Cleo was a world-champion crossword puzzle solver, at least in her mother's mind. While she was searching for a five letter word for "kick," her mother decided to bring up stressful things, which Cleo really didn't want to talk about because, in Cleo's opinion, the best way to deal with stress was to ignore it.

"Cleo, why don't you go out and do things with people? You don't need to worry about me."

Cleo chewed at the end of the eraser, and pretended a keen interest in the crossword. "Mom, I have a busy life. The city takes up most of my time."

"I take up most of your time."

"Do not," Cleo protested, solving the puzzle and switching her attention to the weekend's weather forecast. Rain. They usually walked in the park, her mother loved her walks in the park. With rain, that was out.

"You spend too much time cooped up here."

At that, Cleo knew she should nip the issue in the bud. "It's not true. I've spent exactly four hours with you today, Mom. I got home at eight. It's now nearly midnight. Four. Hours. I'm telling you. The city is killer. You know I spend all my time there. Don't worry about a thing."

"I don't want you giving up something for me, Cleo. Elliott's told me that I might need to move into a home." Now it was her mother's turn to look carefully at the television. *And people wondered where Cleo got it from.* "If that's what you need to do, I'd understand."

"I don't need to do anything. I'm fine, Mom. You're fine. Uncle Elliott and I are handling things fine." Tomorrow she was going to talk to her uncle. He shouldn't have gone behind Cleo's back. They were doing fine.

Her mother folded her hands in her lap and let out a

tired sigh. "You love your job, don't you? I'm very proud of you, Cleo. I don't tell you that often enough, but I want you to know how I feel about you. You've been a good daughter to me, taking care of me, even if you don't want to admit it."

"Why are you telling me this, Mom? Let's watch television, hmm?" She didn't like it when her mother sounded like that, as if she was saying goodbye.

"I think I'm sleepy. I'll go to bed," her mother said, grabbing Cleo's hand for a moment, and Cleo held on a little longer than necessary. Maybe it wasn't the best situation in the world, but it was the best that Cleo could do.

After tucking in her mom, Cleo went back to her room and checked in with the office, processing the e-mail and endless voice mails. There were two urgent e-mails from Bobby and one from her secretary about her schedule for the following week. Next up was voice mail, and that was when she found the message from Sean, telling her how much he liked the way she handled the Town Hall meeting. There were some women who got hot and bothered from hearing how great their hair looked, or how soft their skin felt. Cleo was not one of them.

However, right now, listening to Sean tell her how great she'd been in the meeting, she was drooling in places that ladies weren't supposed to drool. Well, they were, but they weren't supposed to admit it publicly.

Cleo listened once. She listened twice and then she told herself that it was geeky to sit here, playing it over and over, so she brushed her teeth and climbed into bed, where she immediately listened to the message another four times.

Seriously geeky.

Of course, it would be seriously geekier to leave him

a message back. And so, because it was nearly one in the morning, she did.

"Hi. It's Cleo. Got your message. I'm sorry that you suffer from the deluded belief that you're going to derail the sanitation facility because it's not going to happen. New York is number one in the U.S. in trash generation. Did you know that?

"A park is a lovely idea, so pretty and green and full of happy people holding hands and taking long walks, but you and I both know that that's not the world we live in. The world is full of trash, Sean. So I applaud your botanically minded nature, but you're going to lose. Prepare yourself.

"However, that's not why I called. Thank you for the nice words about the meeting. It was difficult with you standing there, watching me, and I kept thinking about what I would do if we were alone, and you kept looking at me as if we were alone, and suffice it to say, it was difficult to keep myself focused, although honestly, I think people were catching on a little at the end.

"I should stop talking now, before I get carried away and tell you what I'm wearing or what I'm not wearing, or where I'm touching myself or what I'm thinking....

"Wish you were here."

After being left alone by his brothers, Sean headed for his apartment, but didn't dare go straight to bed, where he would be tormented by nightmares where Cleo was married and taunting him with it, or the other, more painful images, where she was splayed out beneath him, with ripe milk-white breasts and the red silk of her hair spilling over his pillow.

Instead he made four cups of instant coffee and studied the video depositions for the plaintiff, thinking that nothing would take his mind off sexual frustration like several hours of medical terminology and statistical analysis of risk factors.

Didn't work.

Dr. Howard Phillips, world-renowned kidney specialist testified about the successful usage of peritoneal dialysis, and why a transplant might not be considered medically necessary. All sounded legit. Somewhat damaging to the defendant, New York General, who had pushed Mutual Insurance to pay for the plaintiff's transplant rather than dialysis, but still legit.

Sean was still hard.

Dr. Colbert, California's pre-eminent diagnostic surgeon, droned on about the testing of glomerulonephritis. Weak, very very weak. Sean had seen Dr. Colbert on the stand before.

Rent-a-doc.

Unfortunately, Sean could still feel her grinding against his cock.

So by 5:00 a.m., he had written up his analysis of Dr. Colbert's testimony, suggesting that, under the standard of Daubert, the testimony should be excluded, all while visualizing a weak, wet, desperately panting Cleo poised naked underneath him.

Damn, he was good.

The next morning, he went to the office to pick up some papers that one of the paralegals had left for him, and there he noticed the blinking voice mail light on his phone.

Odds were strong that it was Bruce, leaving another neurotic message for him, but Sean listened to it anyway, on the off chance that yes, maybe…

…it was Cleo.

Sean listened, smiled, then grinned. Now all he could

think about was Cleo, poised naked underneath him, all while touching herself. Sean was nothing if not imaginative. He leaned back in his office chair. Okay, he would be wearing a titanium-steel hard-on for the next twenty-four hours, but this time, the pain would be worth it.

"CLEO, SEAN HERE.

"You have a very confident attitude for someone who's going to be outmaneuvered. You should know that I'm an expert at outmaneuvering. I took a look at the plans. I don't think the sanitation facility needs all that space, do you? Did you see the size of the signage out front? Do you think we need a twelve-by-twenty-four-foot block of marble that tells the world that this is a trash plant? I don't think so. Take off the twelve by twenty-four, shave another thirty feet off the parking facilities, and I think we're nearly there. A little here, a little there, and before you know it, boom, there are trees and flowers and people are taking long walks, holding hands.

"However, that's not why I called. I thought about you last night. Tried to work because my trial starts next week, but I kept getting distracted. You shouldn't have started on the whole sex track because I had told myself not to go down the sex track this weekend since I wasn't going to see you, and by the way, why can't I see you? You never told me. I was thinking, oh, you had plans with your friends. Or maybe a trip up to Albany for business? Only curious…anyway, so I wasn't thinking about sex much—comparatively—until you left the sly little message about what you wear or do not wear to bed. You are the devil, aren't you? So now I have to know: what's your favorite thing to wear to bed?

"Night."

"Sean,

"Cleo here. I looked at the plans, and yes, we could lose the sign, although the architect will hate you and I wouldn't put him first on the list if you needed any sanitation plants designed, because he was very proud of that sign. The parking is another issue. There are ordinances governing parking requirements for buildings. City employees expect city buildings to follow city ordinances. Makes us look sloppy if we don't. You get high marks for creativity, but alas, you have run into a brick wall, or a brick parking lot, if I'm so inclined to make light of seeing someone who's so completely sure of himself taken down. Not that I am, of course.

"However, that's not why I called.

"You asked what my favorite thing was to wear in bed? *"You."*

"Cleo,

"I hate you, and you will pay for this misery. Pay dearly.

"Good night.

"And don't think I didn't notice how you dodged my question about what you're doing this weekend, other than leaving me sordid voice mails that have turned my balls a scary shade of blue. However, that doesn't mean I want you to stop."

7

MONDAY WASN'T SUPPOSED to be perfect. It wasn't supposed to be even close to perfect. Two people having sex on a bench at lunchtime in a long-forgotten subway station was supposed to be cheap and sordid. It was two people scratching an itch and *nothing more,* but from the moment she spotted him waiting for her in the lobby of City Hall, she felt different. She wasn't Cleopatra, the woman whom no man could satisfy. She was Cleo Hollings, the girly-girl who needed to be touched, kissed, adored. For a woman whose ego was large you couldn't send a vibrator to do a man's job. Cleo greedily wanted the whole package.

Today she had brought out all the usual defenses. Black leather coat, stylish leather boots that showed off her legs, a subtle mix of intimidation and sexual innuendo.

When his eyes raked over her, all thoughts of intimidation left her brain.

"You're late," she said, starting on the offensive. He was four minutes and thirty-seven seconds late, and she hated to be kept waiting. *Hated it,* but she suspected he knew.

"Miss me?" he asked casually, meeting her gaze, and she knew he was testing out his own subtle mix of intimidation as well. The heat in his eyes contradicted the casualness of his voice, and Cleo felt the flames start to burn at her skin.

Primed lust was waiting in his eyes. Cleo loved sex, but sex had never given her this buzz in her head, this shock to her nerves. So much coiled tension inside her, all because of the way he watched her.

Slowly they walked down the stairs as if there was all the time in the world. Neither was willing to show anything. She would not give him the satisfaction of knowing how much she wanted this, and oh, she wanted this, she was dying for this. In her head she counted the steps, each beat of her heart firing the pulse between her legs, one step closer to knowing.

One-quarter down, and she could hear the up-tempo in his breathing. Halfway there, and her legs began to shake.

At the last step she waited, poised there. Sean took a ragged breath, and they never made it to the bench. He dragged her against the wall and pushed up her skirt, and raised her leg around his waist.

"Condom?" she gasped, because if he didn't have one (like she really believed that) then she did.

"Already taken care of," he said, and then shoved deep, deep, *deep* inside her.

Oh.

Cleo whimpered. First with the burning pain of being stretched so tight, and then the pain disappeared, leaving only the burn.

Cleo closed her eyes, clenching her muscles around him, around the feel of hard, thick uncontrolled man. *Uncontrolled man.* Sure, he could pretend, but she knew. No man could fake this. She wasn't the only one with weaknesses.

"Very…good," she managed, because she didn't want to tell him how excellent this felt, but then she couldn't talk because he was filling her again and again and again. Her hands grabbed at his shoulders, holding there, feeling his body shake, feeling all that power surging through him. Into her.

It wasn't supposed to be like this. It wasn't supposed to feel so good. So life-alteringly good. This was her hot orgasm, nothing more. She had no heart, he had no heart.

It wasn't supposed to be like this, but it was.

Weakly, her head fell against the wall, and Cleo blindly followed the lead of his hips, caught up in bliss. Heedless, mindless, forgetful bliss.

His fingers tangled in her hair, yanking her mouth up to his, and his tongue and his sex moved in concert, and Cleo was going to burn up in flames. Every time he moved, sensation ripped through her, each thrust a little harder, a little deeper than the last.

Breathing was impossible.

And then he began to talk. Whispering words coarse and raw, promising things in explicit detail, and Cleo shivered, her body clenching around him like a glove. She didn't have time for what he promised, and she shook her head. The first white surges of her climax slammed up inside her, pushing up and up, and she bit her lip because she had wanted this for so long….

It seemed like forever.

His hands moved, shifted underneath her, and she yelled, because his hands were all that was between her and the air and then she felt his finger against her, pressing, and a yell became a groan, became a moan and…

Yes.

As she came, she lost herself in his eyes, the dark brown hypnotizing her, the colors changing, her world spinning. When the world settled again, Cleo raised a hand to his face, touched there, making sure he was real. Her life would be so much easier if this was a dream, but oh, she was glad it was real.

He picked her up and carried her over to the bench. She climbed on top of him, not shy at all.

Sean looked around, shaking his head. "Whose bright idea was it to meet down here?"

"You wanted to see it," she reminded him, feeling his sex, inordinately pleased he was ready again.

"That was Friday. Come to my apartment," he said, lowering her hips onto his with a satisfied sigh. "You do that, and I forget where I am."

"But we can meet here," she said, because an apartment, a hotel, an office, any of those places implied something more than sex. It implied two people who wanted to hold each other, lie together, talk, share secrets.

Still, there in the old station, as he held her, as he filled her, this was something more than sex. She could feel him inside her, reordering her body, reordering her life. Quickly she undid his shirt, finding the skin there, branding it hers.

"How was your weekend?" he asked, shoving up inside her.

Cleo bit her lip, words nearly slipping out. "You're good."

"I can be better. What did you do?"

"Talked on the…phone."

He twisted around and lowered her to the bench, climbing on top of her, hitting his head in the process. "We should be at my apartment."

"Can't," she managed as he ravaged her neck with his mouth, unfastening the buttons of her blouse.

"You could," he said, trailing down lower to her breast, biting gently.

"Can't," she whispered, her tongue in his ear.

He shuddered. "How much time do you have?"

"Twenty minutes left. The clock is ticking."

FREE BOOKS OFFER

To get you started, we'll send you
2 FREE books and a FREE gift

- -

There's no catch, everything is **FREE**

Accepting your 2 **FREE** books and **FREE** mystery gift
places you under no obligation to buy anything.

Be part of the Mills & Boon® Book Club™ and receive your favourite
Series books up to 2 months before they are in the shops and delivered
straight to your door. Plus, enjoy a wide range of **EXCLUSIVE** benefits!

- Best new women's fiction – delivered right to
  your door with FREE P&P

- Avoid disappointment – get your books up to
  2 months before they are in the shops

- No contract – no obligation to buy

We hope that after receiving your free books you'll
want to remain a member. But the choice is yours.
So why not give us a go? You'll be glad you did!

Visit millsandboon.co.uk to stay up to date
with offers and to sign-up for our newsletter

2 **FREE** books
and a
FREE gift

K9JI9

Mrs/Miss/Ms/Mr   Initials

BLOCK CAPITALS PLEASE

Surname

Address

Postcode

Email

MILLS & BOON®
Pure reading pleasure

The Mills & Boon® Book Club™ – Here's how it works:

Accepting your free books places you under no obligation to buy anything. You may keep the books and gift and return the despatch note marked "cancel". If we do not hear from you, about a month later we'll send you 3 brand new books including a 2in1 title priced at £4.99* and two single titles priced £3.19*each. That is the complete price – there is no extra charge for post and packaging. You may cancel at any time, otherwise we will send you 4 stories a month which you may purchase or return to us – the choice is yours.

*Terms and prices subject to change without notice.

NO STAMP
NEEDED!

MILLS & BOON®
Book Club

FREE BOOK OFFER
FREEPOST NAT 10298
RICHMOND
TW9 1BR

NO STAMP
NECESSARY
IF POSTED IN
THE U.K. OR N.I.

"You're going to kill me," he said, and he thrust faster and harder and she couldn't talk anymore and she didn't want to talk anymore. She only wanted to feel.

Her muscles contracted, once, twice, and slowly she regained her breath, savoring the moment of climaxing underneath one Sean O'Sullivan.

Afterwards, he stayed there, their bodies still joined, his finger twisting idly in her hair. She liked the fast rise and fall of his chest against her. These moments were what she feared, yet this was what she craved. When they were together like this, even here, on a hard bench hidden underneath the city, she felt like someone new, someone different, someone happy and content.

"Louise knows something about the bar," she told him, remembering that there was an actual purpose to this meeting, besides the sex. "She'll be traveling with the mayor later this week. While he's gone, I'll get it reopened. By Friday, your brother will be back in business."

"You have any idea of why they shut it down?" he asked, pressing a slow kiss on her neck.

Cleo nearly giggled and Cleo wasn't a giggler by nature. "Not a clue. But I left some messages for some people. Hopefully I'll get some answers."

He raised his head and met her eyes. "Let me take you out tonight."

"I can't."

Cleo stood and brushed hair out of her face, searching for the ponytail band. Sean lay there on the bench, watching her, and she was struck for a second. He was such a perfect specimen of man. All hard muscles and testosterone. A living, walking orgasm. Her living, walking orgasm.

Regretfully, she sighed.

"What *can* you do, Cleo?"

"Don't start now. Don't ruin this."

He stood, putting his clothes back in order. "We're having sex in the middle of a subway station. It's not easy to dress it up, you know."

"It was great sex," she said, trying to mollify him. She didn't want to argue, but she wasn't going to change her life, either. Not even for great sex.

"Well, yes, it was, but normal people don't do this. They don't trade voice mails at two in the morning."

"I'm not a normal person. You're not a normal person. We do what has to be done, however we can. It's why we're having sex in the middle of a subway station, Sean. It's who we are."

He shook his head, swore. "Are you married? I defended you to Gabe, telling him that you weren't married. I couldn't find a hint of it anywhere in your bio, but if you are, I should know."

She looked at him, hurt. It was supposed to be just sex. Just sex wasn't supposed to hurt. This hurt. "I'm not married."

"I know you told me that, and no, I don't think you lied, but yes, okay, sometimes I think that it's the only thing that makes sense, Cleo. It's my job to figure out when people are telling the truth, when they're lying. Sometimes they're not exactly telling the entire truth. You know, you could be separated from your husband, and some people would say, 'no, I'm not married,' when technically they still are, but they believe they're telling the truth…"

She stood, stared at him coldly, silently until he got the message. Cleo might be many bad things, but she wasn't a cheat.

"I'm sorry," he told her, but the wheels were still turning in his head. She could literally see the questions working their way through his brain, processing the evidence against her.

She considered trusting him with the truth about her mother, but he thought she was married, and she thought he was a hot-looking Casanova who took whatever he could. Gee.

Great sex was not a reason for disclosing information that she'd rather keep to herself. And when he looked at her as if he didn't trust her, it was easier to think this was "just sex" after all. "No. I'm not married. I'm not separated. I'm not involved with anyone. There's no reason for you to get all bent out of shape about this."

"Do you have a kid, Cleo? That'd make sense, too. I'm not judgmental or anything. The three of us could have a great time. Go to the movies or something."

"Can you stop with the interrogation, Sean?"

"I want to know."

"I'll tell you. Eventually."

"Why don't you tell me now?"

"We barely know each other."

"That's not true. You're the other half of me."

She stopped abruptly because that was so not fair. "It's a great line, Sean. I bet all the girls really get a kick out of it," she said, her voice dripping with sarcasm.

He didn't even flinch. Most men flinched when she went into full Cleopatra mode. "I know what you're doing, and I'm not going to let you do it."

"What am I doing?"

"You're picking a fight with me, Cleo. It's not going to work."

"Why? Because I haven't fallen in line with your plans yet? Because the bar isn't opened yet? Because when I do, this ride will be over, and you'll send me away happy like every other woman in your life?"

He stood, not saying a word, letting her dump all over him, until slowly her composure returned. It was the first time in her life that Cleo felt ashamed.

"I'm sorry."

"You should be. Don't fight this, Cleo. You don't have to."

He had no idea how scary he was. It was so much nicer and safer if he was a shark, a shyster, a user of women. *They* weren't threats to her, but this…this niceness, this humanity made her weak. Cleo couldn't afford weak.

"We can do breakfast tomorrow."

Cleo wavered, tempted. "I don't know."

"You're free until ten."

"How do you know my schedule?"

"Your secretary is my friend now. She thinks you need a man in your life."

This was why he was so dangerous. Taking all her standard defenses and shredding them to bits. "Breakfast. I'll meet you here. You can bring bagels."

He took her hand, lifted it to his lips. "No. We're going someplace proper."

"We can't have sex?" she asked, hugely disappointed.

He sighed, his shoulders falling. "You're making this very difficult, Cleo."

"I didn't mean to," she said, a total lie and he knew it.

"No sex for breakfast. Unless…"

"Unless what?"

His eyes turned wicked. "I'll make you breakfast at my place. Egg, bacon and sex. You'll be at work by ten, well fed and nicely sated, a bonus all the way around."

Oh, this was going to be tough. She bit her lip, thinking that yes, she could do this. She could do this. "I'll do it," she told him.

He gave her a kiss on the mouth. "See? How hard was that?"

"We're having an affair," she told him, clarifying, because communication was important, lest there be misunderstandings. "We're having an affair."

He looked at her and grinned. "No, we're having breakfast."

LATER THAT MONDAY AFTERNOON, Cleo spent her time running from a meeting to a press conference and back to a meeting in the building department. Work was good, keeping her mind from getting distracted. She'd agreed to a date, technically it was a date with sex (she was no fool), but still, a date. She hadn't been out on a date in nearly four years, and she'd forgotten the pit-in-the-stomach feeling, the checking-the-watch countdown and the endless looks in the mirror to make sure she wasn't getting a zit.

It was pathetic. She made some notes, jotted down a few meaty sound bytes for the mayor and checked her reflection in one of the conference room windows.

Seriously pathetic.

After she left, she spotted Ron Mackey in the hallway. They had spent a few years working together when she was at the department of public housing, and he was a stand-up guy with earnest blue eyes, and a twitchy smile. However, he did have good shoulders. And there was one other thing about him that interested her.

"Ron, you once worked at McFadden Burnett, didn't you?"

Ron looked at her, surprised. "Yeah. I interned there before graduation and then did a couple of years in the coal mines after college."

"Did you know Sean O'Sullivan?"

Ron laughed at that. "Oh, yeah."

"What does that mean?"

The earnest blue eyes looked right through her. "Does he want something from you?"

Cleo met that earnest blue gaze square on. "Not me. It's a friend of mine, actually."

"You *have* friends?" he teased.

"Shut up, Ron, or I'll tell people about that one night five years ago, when you couldn't hmm-hmm-hmm... Is that what you want people to know about you?"

He sighed. "See, this is why you don't have friends. Why do people never have dirt on you?"

"Teflon, baby, I'm made of Teflon. That, and too many people owe me favors. Speaking of, tell me about Sean O'Sullivan."

"He's a good guy, he really is, but you have to watch him, because he's a user. Has a great rep in the firm. They love him because he knows everybody and somehow he seems to win a lot of cases. Big, expensive cases, and the partners really like that. You know, it's funny, he's one of the luckiest guys I ever met. Either that, or one of the slickest. Tell your friend to be careful."

It wasn't what she wanted to hear, but it was what she *needed* to hear. Over and over, everyone said the same thing. Sean was good at getting people to do what he wanted, good at getting women to fall all over him, and Cleo was more than halfway indoctrinated into the Sean O'Sullivan fan club.

She looked at Ron and shrugged. "I've already told her to be careful, but she's a bonehead, and sometimes she doesn't listen to me. Thanks."

He looked at her and shrugged. "You know, that one night was a fluke. I don't always—"

Cleo interrupted before he got too optimistic. "Don't think it, Ron. I don't give second chances."

And in rare circumstances, she wouldn't give first chances, either. From the start, her gut had told her she couldn't keep Sean O'Sullivan in the same category as any other man she'd slept with. Her gut was right. He was adding to her frustration level, her stress level, taking her mind away from things that were important, like her mother, her job. Yes, it was tempting, but no, she wasn't going to take a chance.

"Cold, Cleo. Very cold."

She pulled on her coat, ready to go home. "I know."

THAT EVENING, SHE STAYED UP late, watched *Letterman* with her mother, made her tea and cookies and then retired to her bedroom, where she made the call.

She'd been dreading this all evening, but this wasn't a voice-mail call, this was a person-to-person call.

He picked up right away, and Cleo started talking first. She had to talk first, get it over with, rip the bandage off.

"I'm not going to meet you. I can't do this."

"Why not?"

Why not? Because she spent too much time thinking about him, because he made her want things that she was better off not wanting, because when she was with him she started to doubt her ability to take care of her mother. Any one of those reasons was good enough by itself, but put them all together, and for Cleo, it was disaster.

However, she had another neatly packaged excuse already planned that was close enough to the truth to satisfy her and probably satisfy him. "You said it yourself, Sean. You're the other part of me. You're demanding, forceful, someone that takes from a relationship. Just. Like. Me. At some other time, that might have worked, but I can't. I don't have any of me left to give to someone else. I'm not looking for a relationship, and if I was it'd be with someone else. Someone who doesn't make demands of me, things that I'm not willing to give up."

He laughed at her, not the reaction she had expected. "What sort of drugs are you on, Cleo? You'd get bored in a second. Less than a second."

Okay, he didn't believe her neatly packaged excuse. Not a problem. "I can't, Sean."

"You can't do this to me, Cleo. You have to give me some sort of reason. Something that makes sense."

"I'm not in a place where I can do what you'd want me to do," she answered vaguely, really wishing he wasn't a lawyer.

"What the hell does that mean?"

Cleo's stomach was tied in knots, her blood pressure was up, and she knew she was making the right decision. She didn't need all this emotional upheaval. She couldn't handle it anymore. "It means you want normal, you want 24/7, you want to change my life, and I'm not letting anybody change my life."

"Are we talking about your job, Cleo? I think your job is great. I think it's beyond great."

He sounded so well-adjusted, just like Danny had sounded, right before he kicked her out of his life. But Cleo was smarter this time. "When the demands really start kicking in, you'd want me to give up things. That's the way people are. They think everything will be fine at the beginning, but then, when you have to sacrifice things, when you spend some nights alone, it won't be so great anymore, Sean."

"I thought we were only having an affair. That's what you keep telling me, Cleo. Oh, yeah, this is nothing. It sounds like a lot more than an affair. I think you're running scared. I think you're a coward."

Instantly, Cleo saw red. "A coward? Oh, yeah right. Most people wouldn't have the guts to do what I'm doing, did you know that? I may be a lot of bad things, but I'm not a coward. Go to hell, Sean. And good night."

She hung up, ending the conversation on a low note.

She stared at her cell phone, waiting for him to call back, but she knew he wouldn't. Sean O'Sullivan didn't give second chances, either. Not that she wanted one, of course.

No, she'd made the right decision, she said to herself, curling up with her phone under her pillow.

Just in case.

8

SEAN TRIED TO SLEEP. It was impossible. He tried to work. That was impossible as well. Next step, call Gabe.

"What are you doing?"

"It's two a.m. I'm sleeping."

"Oh."

"What's wrong, Sean?"

"I think I've been dumped."

"Think?" Gabe asked, his voice coming alert.

"She said she didn't want to see me again. Why does a woman say that?"

"Because she doesn't want to see you again. What did you do?"

"I. Did. Nothing. I was perfect. Picture-perfect. Not a mistake made, not one misstep. It was textbook, Gabe. Textbook."

"Is this the married one?"

"She's not married. I got one of the firms P.I.'s to find out what's going on. Soon I'll know the truth."

"The truth is that she's married. She had an attack of conscience."

There was a click and then a female voice came on the line. "Sean? Why are you calling at two a.m.?"

"Tessa?"

"Yes."

"Sean got dumped," Gabe said.

"No kidding?"

"I didn't get dumped."

"Oh, excuse me. She doesn't want to see him again, which means, hmm, let me guess, dumped."

"Wow. That's so wrong. I think you're better off without her." At least Tessa was on Sean's side, demonstrating some much-deserved sympathy.

"I know I'm better off without her. Of course I'm better off without her. I mean, she's a total case. Cranky, hot tempered, workaholic and this great mouth that can rip you a new one without thinking about it twice."

"She's all that and she's actually married?" asked Tessa doubtfully.

"She's not married."

"I think she's married," chimed Gabe.

Tessa sighed. "You think everyone should be married, Gabe, but the truth is that marriage is merely a piece of paper."

"It's a sign of commitment, Tessa."

"I'm committed. I love you, Gabe."

"I know that—"

"Excuse me? Can we talk about me for a minute?"

"Oh, sure. Sean, go to sleep. She's either married or a total witch, and either way, you're better off without her."

"I like her," he said quietly.

"Why?" Tessa asked.

"She's loyal and intense and strong. Really tough."

Cleo fascinated him like no other woman had. Maybe he had some long-repressed masochist tendencies inside him, but truthfully, he'd never met a woman who was that strong before. Sean wanted to own her, probably not politically correct, but deep in his heart, Sean didn't have a PC bone in his body.

"I'm sorry, Sean, but you'll meet someone else. You have to find the one perfect person for you—"

"And then you should marry them," inserted Gabe.

"Gabe..." said Tessa, huffing. "What am I going to do with you?"

"I *could* give you some ideas."

There was a long—painfully long—silence.

"Excuse me? I'm hurting here. Can we talk about Sean for a minute?"

And for the second time that night, the phone went dead.

Hell.

FOR THREE DAYS, Cleo suffered in the black misery of her own making, which only made it more miserable. Somehow misery was more palatable when someone else could be blamed for it, but this time the blame was all hers.

Her blood pressure tripled, her secretary was giving her lectures on proper office protocol, and yesterday in the press conference with the president of El Salvador, she'd forgotten his name. Not the finest moment in U.S.-El Salvador relations. Her three interns had started to flee when she approached, and she was approaching Thursday, the next scheduled Town Hall meeting on the park project, with an odd sense of fear and hope.

Fear that she would do something really stupid, like explain to him how idiotic she'd been and tell Sean that she'd made a mistake, which she had admitted only twice before in her life and both times were before the age of ten. And her solitary hope was that he'd use all that persuasive guile to seduce her right back into doing something really stupid. She had all the usual mentally debilitating qualms, time-consuming worries and confidence-popping obsessions of being in a relationship, without the fun of being in a relationship. It truly sucked.

And it all hit home—literally—when she came home late on Wednesday night, having spent the entire day planning for the moment that she'd see Sean again.

When she unlocked the door, she was hit with the savory aroma of beef stroganoff.

Dinner.

Uncle Elliott appeared in the doorway to the kitchen, spoon in hand.

She had promised to cook dinner.

She had forgotten.

Being Cleo was sometimes, like now, a curse. She was never content with second place, though the position of Deputy Mayor was okay for now, one day she'd be ready to run for mayor herself. She had mastered the art of quirking one eyebrow by practicing in the mirror for seven hours straight, until she got it perfect.

When she did things, she jumped in feet first, no looking. And when she did Sean, she jumped in feet first, no looking, and she should have looked. She had tried to look. She had wanted to look, but she didn't.

And now here she was.

Forgetting about the dinner she had promised to cook.

Her uncle didn't appear mad, which made it worse. "How was your day?" he asked.

"Busy. Sorry," she said, draping her coat on the coat tree, then planting a kiss on her mother's forehead.

"Hello, Mom."

Her mother frowned, confused. "Margaret?"

"No, Mom."

Her uncle came into the room. "It hasn't been a good day," he said.

The good days were becoming more and more rare, special treats to be savored and celebrated, and Cleo looked at her mother and smiled.

"I can take over if you want."

"No worries, Cleo. I've got everything under control."

And he did. Her uncle. Her seventy-year-old uncle who managed apartments during the day had everything under control.

In bed that evening, she tossed and turned, checking her voice mail four times just in case, but there was nothing. And then she did the one thing that Cleo never did—reconsidered. Not one thing was working in her life at the moment. Not the situation with her mother, not her job and not Sean.

The next morning, she got dressed for work, slowly, silently beaten. She didn't wear power-hugging black, or self-confident red, instead she went for demure, nervous, self-conscious pink. Which was Cleo's way of saying she was wrong, not that Sean would be able to figure that out by her attire; no, she'd have to help him figure it out. She'd have to use those words that she never uttered, except for the two times before she turned ten, and both times she'd been under severe emotional distress (i.e., being grounded for the next five months) unless she admitted the truth.

There were similarities.

"I'm wrong," she said to the mirror, practicing, rehearsing and hating the whole experience, but she'd have to suck this up, because the alternative (i.e., continuing to go without him) was ten times worse.

She'd been wrong to tell Sean that she couldn't see him again, when she wanted nothing more than to see him again, have sex with him again, possibly—probably trade voice messages with him again, touch him again, let him hold her again, kiss her again…and, well, she could go on with the "agains" because there were really too many of them, and they all kept bombarding her at the worst possible time.

She'd known him for exactly one week, but she felt as if she'd known him all her life. He'd been right. He was the other part of her and she missed that part.

Cleo missed Sean.

Missed the cocky smile. Missed the killer thighs. Missed the way his eyes narrowed when he started thinking devious thoughts. Missed the way his devious mind worked.

Missed. Him.

And even though she hadn't told him yet, she was prepared to be gracious and conciliatory. Show him, in the most saving-face way possible (i.e. in public), that she wanted to start over, if only so she wouldn't have to listen to him lord it over her because she knew he would, and she really hated when people did that, and she suspected that Sean would be more gloating than most.

Finally, the moment of truth arrived. Cleo dressed humbly in her light pink blazer, with matching heels. And okay, yes, the heels were three-inch killers, but this was not the Wicked Witch of Murray Street. This was definitely Jackie O. Gracious, ladylike, elegant— yet still hugely confident—Jackie O.

The room was as crowded as before, but this time, Sean was standing near the back, arms crossed across his chest, face guarded. In fact, he looked so guarded that he probably wasn't going to discern her change of position easily.

Darn.

Cleo began the same way as before, soothing ruffled feathers, showing concern for the citizens, etc, etc, etc, not looking in his direction once. However, eventually she got to the part where Cleo admitted she was wrong:

"I took a look at the plans, and I think there's a little room—"

"There's a lot of room." The voice came from the petite, blue-eyed blonde who was sitting on the sidelines. *In pink.*

Cleo turned to her. "Yes?"

"After Mr. O'Sullivan called and asked me so nicely, we took another look at the plans, and there's a lot of room for modification."

Mr. O'Sullivan? Cleo fumed, apparently fuming out loud, because the pink vision answered.

"Sean," the vision said lovingly, with one of those cute little homecoming princess smiles that Cleo had never mastered. "I think we can get the West Side Ladies Botanical Preservation Group exactly what they want. It won't be huge, but I've talked to my boss—"

"And who exactly is your boss?" interrupted Cleo, because humble pink was boiling over to death-match red—symbol of the death and destruction of Cleo's one shining, albeit short, moment in humility.

"I work for Douglas Atwater, department of sanitation. I manage the construction projects for the department."

Instantly, Cleo's gaze shot to Sean. She shouldn't have looked, but she had to know if all these paranoid thoughts in her brain were correct. He'd gone to someone else and seduced them to his side? One look at the granite-hard smile and she knew: Deus ex machina had absolutely nothing on Sean O'Sullivan's behind the scenes bedwork.

For a second she struggled to breath. Eventually, she got her composure back. Hopefully no one noticed. "Miss— Excuse me, what did you see your name was?"

"Serena. Serena Dimon."

Serena. The city of New York was now being run by a tiny blond woman named Serena. "You know, go ahead. I'll sit back and listen," said Cleo in soothing constituent voice, and there was only one other person in the room who would pick up on her sarcasm. Sean, because he would recognize the tone for what it was.

For the next fifteen minutes, the audience was captivated by the images that one Serena Dimon was painting of a West Side dockland that was teeming with flowers and trees, singing bluebirds and rainbow-colored unicorns that frolicked in the woods nearby.

Each second that passed, Cleo's mood grew fouler, and her smile broadened in a purely defensive manner. There was a bloodless coup on the horizon. Cleo was being outted—from the meeting and from Sean's life—replaced by a vivacious five-foot-two princess from the happiest kingdom on earth, with perky blue eyes and breasts that were most likely plasticoid (not jealous).

Serena finished, turned worshipful eyes to Sean (not jealous) and giggled. Cleo was ready to hurl, but nobody was going to know because, when push came to shove, Cleo could hide her emotions along with the best of them.

"That's great," she purred.

Sean raised a hand and she smiled as she pointed at him, beamed, grinned brighter than Broadway, because Cleo was going to be happy, *happy.* "You have the floor, Mr. O'Sullivan." *Prince of Darkness, Corrupter of Women and Heathenish Snatcher of Candy from Babies.*

"It sounds like we can come to consensus after all," he quipped, which was lawyer-talk for "screw you."

"There was never any doubt in my mind," Cleo lied sweetly. No doubt about it, he was a world-class bastard capable of ripping out beating hearts with one hand tied behind his back.

"You look pleased," he said, rubbing salt into the wound.

Pleased? "I'm always pleased when people come to me with solutions rather than problems, and the fact that my people are willing to go the extra mile for the West Side Ladies Botanical Preservation Group, well, golly, that's just a bonus." *An even larger bonus would be an anvil falling on your head and crushing your skull, with your brains oozing... No, inappropriate.*

"You're calling this a solution, then? You didn't think this park was possible before. Now it is?"

I'll take your heart, lay it out in the desert for the vultures to feed on... NO, inappropriate.

She cleared her throat. "I think Serena is going to make this park more than possible for you, and everyone else, of course. Such dedication. Above and beyond the call of duty."

"No hard feelings?" he drawled.

Oh, no, he didn't. Oh, no, he didn't. He did not just say that.

For one long, long second, she considered letting him know exactly how hard her feelings currently were, but that would be "unprofessional," so Cleo smiled. "Already forgotten. I think I'll go back to my office and look at the plans again." *And shove a dagger through your cold, black heart.*

Not jealous. Not jealous at all.

WOUNDED MALE PRIDE is a savage beast, the impetus of untold human disasters throughout the centuries. The cause of wars, of political upheaval, of moments when men must look back and ask themselves, "Why the hell did I just do that?"

Sean looked at Cleo's departing back, thinking it was strangely ironic that the Deputy Mayor of New York, a woman rumored to have no heart, had the most perfect heart-shaped ass on the entire planet. Such contradictions confused him, baffled him and, sadly, obsessed him. Sean sighed.

He had thought this little charade would help him get over her. Sadly, it only made it worse.

She had taken it on the chin, but didn't flinch, didn't wince, didn't even have the decency to glare at him once with those hot amber eyes. Only her soothing constituent voice (patently false) had told him that he'd hit a nerve.

"Did it work?" asked Serena, finding him after the meeting was over.

"Did it restore my love life to its rightful order? No. Did it help my wounded pride? Hell, no. You did great, Serena. Thanks. Tell Robert hello, and we'll have to go out for drinks one of these nights. I owe him."

Serena patted his arm as if he was losing his mind. He was. "I'm sorry, Sean. But Cleo? I mean, come on."

"You know her?" he asked, because he was fast learning that although everybody knew "of" Cleo, very few people *knew* her.

"Only by reputation. Douglas really likes working for her, but he doesn't tell anybody because he's afraid the guys will laugh at him. I think it's hard for a lot of these tough, old-school men to work for a woman. But they seem to have an understanding. The men grumble and complain about her and Cleo lets them."

Sean shook his head.

"What are you going to do?"

"Hell if I know."

IT WAS LESS THAN thirty minutes later when Sean appeared at her office door. Her eyes drank him in because she was a weak female who had no pride anymore and was currently wearing pink. A low moment in her life.

She stood, using the desk like a shield, not telling him to leave, which, if she was smart, she would.

Sean closed the door, then plunked down two round ramekins on her desk. "I brought dessert. It wasn't much, but I had no idea what to do, and I knew flowers and candy would only end up in the trash…or the East River…so I thought maybe…crème brûlée."

As if crème brûlée could cure all the world's problems. Right.

She shot him an ominous look, then picked up the ceramic container, wound up in her finest Bronx Bomber style, then threw it across the room, shattering it nicely. Cleo would clean it up later, before the cleaning people wondered why she was throwing custard in her office, but right now, she needed that satisfaction.

Her battered heart felt better—somewhat.

Sorrowfully Sean looked at the mess on the floor. "Okay, maybe crème brûlée wasn't the best idea. Today was an act. Meant to make you jealous."

"An *act?* And that is supposed to make me feel better?"

Amazingly, it did. Relief came over her in huge waves, but it wasn't enough for Cleo, who had just been shown up by little Miss West Side Princess, and she wasn't *happy*.

"Is this an apology?" she asked, noting the careful omission, waving it under his nose. Actions only went so far. Words were so much nicer.

"Doesn't it look like an apology?" he sidestepped in true lawyer fashion.

"The words," she stated firmly, arms crossed firmly over her chest.

"Cleo," he said, advancing in her direction, backing her onto the desk, intent purpose in his eyes.

"You only care about the things you want." She flung the words like a knife thrower because when he looked at her like that, she had the insane desire to be the sort of woman in pink who would let the sin go unpunished. As if. "The bar, the park—"

"You," he said, still closer, almost touching her. She wanted his hands on her. He wanted his hands on her. It was there in his face, his eyes, the hard line twisting his mouth, the hard line tenting his slacks. Her body was already arching, anticipating, but that last statement caught her undivided attention with its blatant untruthfulness. Wanting her was one thing, caring another, and she recognized the difference.

"Wanting is not caring. I'm not nice. I'm mean, slightly shrewish, and although I do have nice qualities as well, on the whole—"

He interrupted her with a kiss.

Sean kissed her like she wasn't mean, like she wasn't slightly shrewish, like he wanted to be with her. Her, the Wicked Witch of Murray Street.

Her arms (not stupid) brought him closer, and she kissed him back like she wasn't mean or slightly shrewish until he lifted his head, his eyes gloating, but in the very best sort of way. "I needed that."

"I'll take that as an apology," she said magnanimously, because her lips were still pumped, he was still holding her, and she could afford it. Just this once.

"Your turn," he said, stepping back, not holding her, expecting…

"What?" she asked, hoping he would have forgotten.

"Have you forgotten your complicity in all this? I would not have been driven to desperate measures—

desperate measures," he repeated, with a courtroom flourish, "if you hadn't decided you were going to throw me out of your life."

Okay, he remembered that small piece.

"I was trying to be honest with you," she said, sidestepping in true political fashion.

"No, you weren't," he answered. "Have you changed your mind about us?"

The moment of truth. Put up or stop whining. Cleo knew it, and she was going to do this. She was going to take care of her mother, run New York and make time for Sean O'Sullivan, too. She was Cleo Hollings. She could do the impossible.

She nodded.

"The words," he prompted.

"I'm sorry," she said. "I was wrong. We'll do it."

"Now was that so hard?"

"It was awful," she muttered. "You?"

"Hated it. Want some crème brûlée?" he asked, holding out the remaining ramekin.

"You trust me not to throw it?"

"Of course."

She stuck a finger in the custard and pulled out a dollop, eyeing it, eyeing him, all the while wicked, wicked thoughts ran thorough her head. Cleo took the cream, took her finger and sucked—indulgently.

Breathless, she waited, and his eyes narrowed—deliciously. He asked, "How much time do you have? If the gods are merciful, you're free for a good…two hours."

She checked the agenda. "I'm supposed to be in a staff meeting in fifteen."

Slowly, torturously, she licked her lips. His dark gaze followed the movement, but she wasn't going to assume. He should know how it would be if they stayed together. This is what he wanted, but it wasn't going to be pretty or relaxing or orderly. She had to live her life in fifteen-minute intervals, grabbing what she could, when she could.

Impatiently, he undid her demure pink blazer, finding black silk hidden beneath, and for a moment his breathing visibly stopped.

Obviously, Sean was going to grab what he could, when he could, too.

Soul mates. Definitely.

"Please tell me you locked the door behind you," she whispered, watching with fevered eyes as he took a dab of the dessert on his finger. Not nearly as impatient this time, he put it in her mouth, and she sucked. Hard. As if her life depended on it, because soon this was going to be a matter of life and death. She needed this. She had dreamed about this. And she was catching fire all over.

She wasn't the only one.

Sean was pitched tight and tense, and she stroked his finger with her tongue, and he groaned—painfully, pulling out his finger, stroking her mouth. His hands brought her closer, spanning her waist, her rear, and he rocked her against him. Their bodies matched perfectly. She could feel his sex, feel all that blood throbbing through him. Waiting, poised, thrilling her.

"Fifteen minutes?" he asked, and she managed to nod once, her hand already busy at his fly.

He smiled, shook his head. "Don't think so."

Then he pushed her back against the desk, took another fingerful of cream and she waited for him to put it into her mouth, but he didn't.

Sean lifted her skirt, stripped off her panties, and she realized exactly where he wanted the dessert. There.

Oh, no he didn't. Oh, no he didn't.

The wicked finger covered her with cream and she blocked out the implications because she was never, *ever* going to look at crème brûlée the same way again.

"Fifteen minutes," she gasped, because there were so many things he would lose out on if he…

Oh.

And he did. Using his mouth, his tongue, he lapped her, loved her, tortured her. Wicked. There was no other word. With each long stroke of his tongue, she forgot and forgave and slowly lost all sense of pretty much everything. It truly was the best sort of apology in the world.

Instinctively her hips rose, and her eyes closed because she was going to come.

Soon. Instantaneously soon, and she told him so. Repeatedly. Furiously. Demandingly.

Sean, not understanding the meaning of the word "soon" was slow and thorough, and she wanted him to hurry because fifteen minutes was really that long, and she wanted this so badly. The orgasm was there, waiting, and each time his mouth touched her, the orgasm grew, like a snowball, gathering speed, gathering size, gathering alarming avalanche potential.

"Sean," she moaned, because they were running out of time, she was running out of brain cells, and she wanted this orgasm. With each stroke, her hold on the world danced one step away.

Firm hands held her down, and she stared, blind, dazed. Her hips began to jerk because he wasn't gentle anymore. He was cruel, merciless, and Cleo was starting to burn, the pressure building inside her, threatening to consume her. She struggled but Sean wasn't going anywhere.

"Please."

"Five minutes," he whispered, the devil himself, and

his mouth tickled her thighs. His hands touched her, and she could feel his finger inside her, pushing, thrusting, and the suckling pressure of his tongue was the best and worst sort of pleasure.

"One minute left," he warned, and her head shifted, her hips bucking, and she needed this, needed him, and his mouth was hard on her, and she knew that their time was nearly up.

He didn't let up, and the climax hit her, sensations rolling over her, and finally, *finally,* Sean raised his head.

He looked at her over the decimated remains of her body, his eyes pleased. "You'd better go, the mayor is waiting."

Furiously, she jerked her clothes in place, and oh, he was all Mr. Polished and Tailored and Happy and Composed, and she'd just ridden through four hurricanes and her knees didn't want to move and the words most likely to emerge from her lips weren't the ones suited for city government, so she glared.

He laughed.

And she smiled in return. "You are the devil."

"Payback is hell, Cleo. Come on. I'll help you walk. No one will ever know. Wicked Witch of Murray Street, my ass. You're a kitten."

She hit him. Maybe she was in pink. Maybe her lower torso felt as if it'd been shattered like tempered glass. Maybe she held on to his arm a little tighter than necessary.

But she was Cleo, and Cleo was back.

9

THAT NIGHT, SEAN CALLED HER. Not her voice mail. Direct person-to-person communication. It was late, after midnight, the apartment was quiet, and instantly she pulled her jangling cell from underneath her pillow.

"Hello?"

"Am I interrupting any of those wild sex dreams again?"

"No," she muttered, not wanting to be embarrassed, having no reason to be embarrassed, but embarrassed, nonetheless.

"It's because your sex life is now improving by leaps and bounds. I told you I'd banish that rat Mark Anthony from your head."

"I think you've missed your calling as a gigolo," she told him, trying to make it sound like an insult. Failing.

"Are you mocking my woman-pleasing abilities, oh, woman who was writhing and moaning and begging and pleading like a...well, like a woman who really needed a world-class orgasm."

"I never beg," she snapped.

"You were begging. You would have been on your knees if you could have moved—beyond the writhing, of course."

"I think we've now more than adequately covered this territory," Cleo responded.

"But you're so much fun to tease, Cleo. Come on. If I can't be there in your bed, slipping inside you, pounding away, deriving hours upon hours of personal satisfaction, do not deny me the momentary, and extraordinarily smaller pleasure of teasing you."

"Hours and hours?" she asked, mildly sarcastic, yet still hopelessly curious.

"There are many ways to pleasure a woman. Do not limit your imagination to only one."

"Oh," she said, chastised.

"But yeah, even in the traditional sense, I could."

Her mouth curved into an unwitting smile. "You are a tease."

"Now that's the Deputy Mayor calling the kettle black. Your eyes light up like New Year's when a man starts panting around you, and I would lay odds—even odds—that other parts of you light up equally bright. Why must you hate men so?"

"I don't hate men. I love men. I think I'd forgotten how much I love men."

"No, you're no lover of men. It's because my woman-pleasing capabilities are influencing your judgment for the positive."

She wanted to continue this all night, talking, teasing, being happy, but she did have a job to do, and she still wasn't completely caught up on her sleep. Under-eye concealer only went so far to cover up the dark circles she'd been sporting. "I should have your brother's bar opened by tomorrow. I've battled the health department, the historical society, the state liquor authority and all that's left is my office, and then the bar will be in the clear. By tomorrow night, he'll be back serving booze, making people happy."

"Thank you."

"You've repaid me enough, Sean."

"Do you think that's why I'm seeing you?" he asked, his voice no longer light.

Cleo thought, long and hard, because she knew what everyone had told her, but her instincts were good. Better than good. "No."

"That's my girl."

Such small words, such a non-small impact on her heart. She wanted to keep this at sex, just sex, but every time she saw him, every time she talked to him, "just sex" was getting to be more difficult. Not the sex, but the "just" part.

"I have to go to work early in the morning."

"I know. I only called to tell you good-night. I wanted to be there, holding you, tasting you and listening to you breathe. Lying here alone, listening to you talk is the only option I have."

"Good night," she answered quickly and then hung up.

Just sex, she reminded herself. It was only really good sex.

Deep inside her, the dark recesses of her heart were pointing and laughing their capillaries off. She was falling for him. Falling hard, falling fast.

Sadly, for Cleo, there wasn't any other way.

SEAN CAME IN EXTRA EARLY the next morning, his D&G tie disgracefully stuffed in his pocket, his hair still shower-wet, intending to perform the work that Bruce overpaid him for. However, he wanted to see Cleo, he was dying to see her, and magically, she was only a stone's throw from the courthouse where, technically, he could relieve a paralegal of his duties and file the Daubert motion himself.

Of course, given the throng of paralegals and runners

he had at his disposal, he hadn't filed a motion himself since he was an intern during law school.

But thirty minutes later, when the sun was just starting to break over the horizon, he found himself in City Hall Park, an oasis filled with hickory trees and curvy black metal benches and iron streetlamps that had been there since the turn of the century. The security fences and police presence were unfortunate and new.

Sean looked up at the big glass window that he knew belonged to Cleo. Not surprisingly, her light was on. Whatever secret kept her home at night didn't keep her from her office in the early morning. His P.I. would have something soon, and his curiosity would be satisfied, but for now…

Sean picked up a large hickory nut and chucked it at her window, where it hit the double-reinforced glass with a satisfying whack.

Immediately a policeman appeared.

"Excuse me, sir, what are you doing?"

Acting like an idiot, but that was something that Sean would never admit publicly. He could see a flash of color at the window, but had no idea if Cleo was actually there or not. "It's a family tradition that we have. It dates back three or four hundred years, I think. A toss for good luck. For some people, it's salt. For us, it's hickory nuts. Before a big case, I come down here, and toss a nut toward the fountain."

"The fountain's in the other direction. That's a window, sir. A window at City Hall."

"I got carried away," he said, noticing Cleo coming down the path through the park, the morning fog making her appear mystical, like something from his dreams. Which was good, because right at this moment, he needed rescuing. He looked at Cleo, shrugged his shoulders casually, as if this was something he did all the time, waiting for her to take charge of the situation. However, she didn't say a word.

"Cleo, you can clear this up," he prodded. "Explain to the officer why I would be throwing a nut at your window."

She looked him over, amber eyes flicking up and down. "Do I know you?"

The officer started to look concerned. "Is there a problem?"

Sean started to feel concerned. "Cleo, this isn't the time for *teasing*."

Her eyes stared right through him. "Am I supposed to understand what you're talking about?"

Okay, this was wrong. She was carrying the charade way too far. "Is this because of last night?" He hadn't done anything wrong. Teased her a little, and she needed teasing. Cleo needed to lighten up, and he was just the guy to do it.

Her arms crossed across her chest. "Sir, I don't think you understand how seriously we take security in this city. The protection of our citizens, our bastions of government are not to be toyed with, nor played with."

"Cleo," he said warningly.

The officer, sensing impending violence, stepped in front of Sean. "Would you like me to take him across the street?"

"You and what army?" scoffed Sean.

"That would be good," answered Cleo, with a tiny, wicked smile and Sean's mouth fell open.

"You can't do that," he protested. "I know my rights."

"I'm the Deputy Mayor, sir. I'm charged with enforcing the laws of this city, and you're in clear violation of New York City Municipal ordinance, Chapter 2, Title 4, Section 407(e), and I quote, 'Pursuant to previously defined Section 407(a), no person shall be allowed to throw, cast, or in any way propel, any projectile, weapon, or object capable of physical harm on municipal property defined in Section 407(d).'"

The policeman put a hand on his arm, Sean shook it off. "Cleo, you can't have me arrested."

She stood, so confident…so hot, and it was wrong for a man facing criminal charges to be thinking about sex. Wrong. Very, very wrong. Slowly, her mouth inched up at one corner. "What's the magic word?"

Sean's hands fisted, but he wisely kept them stuffed in his pockets, lest Policeman Bob get the wrong idea. "It was a nut. A hickory nut. A product of nature. That is not a weapon. A weapon is any object capable of being readily used by one person to inflict severe bodily injury upon another person."

At the mention of severe bodily injury, the officer's expression darkened. "Are you threatening the Deputy Mayor, sir?"

Sean stared at her. "Cleo."

Her smile was gloriously tempting and went straight to his head. The wrong head. "What's the magic word?"

Sean looked at the officer, looked at Cleo, who wasn't going to back down, and knew when to fold. "Please," he muttered, low and under his breath.

"Did you say something, sir? I must have missed it."

"PLEASE," he yelled, sending one of the fat park squirrels running for cover.

"Now isn't it nice when we practice our manners?" She turned to the officer, who was starting to figure things out. "You can go, Tom."

"It's Frank, ma'am."

"Frank, then."

After Frank left, Sean looked at her curiously. "Would you really have had me arrested?"

"You know the law. Do the crime, do the time."

"What was the purpose behind all that?"

"To remind you that I don't beg. Ever."

She'd been begging. It'd been the most erotic thing he'd ever seen, but he was smart enough not to tell her that. Besides, there were better ways for further payback. Funner ways for payback.

He looked at her sideways. "Cleo?"

"Yes?" she said, and he took one step toward her.

Wisely, she backed up, unwisely into the copse of trees.

But he took her mouth, anyway, mostly to remind her that yes, she did beg, and yes, he could make her. She tasted like coffee and toothpaste and all those morning tastes that he should know about—if he ever got to spend any time with her.

Desperately, she kissed him back. *Desperately.* Sean worked her hands behind the tree, keeping them locked there. His brain started to cloud, because whenever she had her tongue in his mouth, his brain didn't work correctly, but this was a matter of survival. There were principles at stake. Battles to be won, wars to wage.

Women didn't do this to Sean. Ever. Not even Cleo, who got more passes than most.

She pressed against him, hips grinding urgently. She didn't beg? Ha.

Arms encircling, he trapped her there with his body, his fingers reaching into his pocket, finding his D&G tie and tying her hands.

As soon as she felt the bonds, she bit his tongue. That really shouldn't have turned him on, *really shouldn't,* but it did.

Sean laughed. "Payback," he whispered against her lips.

"Sean. You have to let me go. I will scream, and the police will come and arrest you. For real, this time."

Her cheeks were flushed, her eyes on fire, and her mouth was still swollen from his. It was almost better than sex. Almost. Honestly, nothing compared to sex with Cleo, and someday, they'd actually have it in a bed.

But for now, his bold fingers delved under her blouse, under her bra, finding flesh, finding skin, finding breasts. He fondled her, her nipples springing to life. "You want to call the cops, like this? It could be worse."

She brought up a knee to his crotch. Hard.

Okay, that was worse.

It took a minute for Sean's eyes to focus. "That was dirty."

"And what do you think *this* is?" she hissed, struggling, hair tossing, and oh, damn, they were really going to have to try this in bed.

"Payback. You do not mess with me, Cleo. You will lose, every time." She needed to know that when it came to fighting dirty, Sean was the master.

She scoffed. "Ha. I am Deputy Mayor of this city. Deputy. Mayor. You think you can win against me? Think again."

He took a step back to admire his handiwork, but something was wrong with this picture. He should have been happy, punching a fist in the air, watching her, finally, *finally,* at his mercy. He had thought that he wanted her on her knees.

"That's not what this is about," he told her, and he realized it wasn't.

"Then what is this about, Sean?"

What did he want? "You were begging yesterday. You said you weren't, but you were, and I want you to admit it. Admit it, and I'll untie you." Still spouting the same party line that he'd started with, but the words were starting to sound shrill to his ears. They sounded wrong.

She stopped struggling and glared. "This is about your *pride*. I am tied up with a…tie, because you cannot stand the idea that I not all 'oh, baby, baby' over you."

"Yes. It's about my pride. Make fun, mock me if you want, but I'm not standing there tied up to a tree." He crossed his arms over his chest, feeling something hollow inside him.

"No," she replied, her eyes magnificently stubborn, and he started to walk away.

One step. Two steps. Two and a half steps. Two and three quarter steps. Farther away from *her.*

This wasn't fun anymore. This wasn't a game. *What the hell was he doing?*

"Sean."

He turned, carefully keeping the anxiety from his eyes.

"I shouldn't have done the thing with the cops. I'm sorry."

"That wasn't what I asked for," he told her. Right then, he knew. There was always a moment when you could look at a witness and see the truth that they hadn't even acknowledged, even to themselves. In the court-room, that was when Sean would shine. He knew how to get at the unwanted truth. Knew the questions to ask, knew the way to twist the knife exactly right to get what he wanted the person to say.

It was his own knife twisting in his gut, and the unwanted truth burst free.

Sean wanted a lot more than an apology. A lot more

than her body. He wanted her heart, and it scared the hell out of him, because he didn't know what he would do if he couldn't have it. She was the strongest woman he'd ever met. It was why he loved her. It was why he didn't want her on her knees. He wanted her by his side, but hell, Sean didn't have a clue how to do this with a normal woman.

Between his emotionally stunted nature and Cleo's usual defenses, which made Rikers look like a playpen, theirs was the apocalypse come to life.

She looked at him, reading all those fears inside him because Cleo knew a man's weakness inherently. That was her talent. "No," she answered, denying him to the end.

It started as such a great plan. All he wanted was for her to acknowledge him, to acknowledge his place in her life.

He loved her.

Yes, it was pride, but he didn't care if she was all "baby, baby." Cleo? Hello? That wasn't what he wanted. Just once, he wanted to know that she experienced the same weak-kneed feelings that he did. To believe that she felt the same desperate ache inside her to be with him, the same painful need to touch.

He'd never loved a woman before, never felt the urge to prostrate himself before her, but with Cleo his pride was zooming out the window with rocket speed. It was painful and pitiful, and Cleo was putting him through hoops that Sean would never have tolerated before.

It was that demeaning lack of pride that made him untie her, the silk fabric falling away to the ground. Bright red, crushed, crumpled.

Damn.

"Sean," she said quietly, all anger gone from her

face. Instead leaving the exact thing he wanted. Cleo Hollings. Vulnerable. Exposed.

"What?" he asked carefully, giving nothing away.

"For you—only you—I would beg."

CLEO SHOULDN'T HAVE told him, but somewhere along the way, she lost her will to fight.

Nervously, she swallowed, waiting for him to gloat, because she knew he would.

He didn't.

Instead, he watched her, dark eyes wary and appraising, before he nodded without a trace of victory at all. "Thank you," he said simply. "I should go. You need to work. I need to work."

"Sean?" she asked, because she wasn't ready for him to go. Not yet.

"Yeah?"

"Do you want to go get a cup of coffee? I have a half hour."

He almost smiled. "That'd be good."

The café was around the corner, with tiny tables and tiny chairs, and no way for two people to talk privately or fight privately or grope privately. So they were going to have to talk publicly. Both novel and necessary.

They ordered coffees and found a table in the back, sardined between a couple of lawyer types who knew Sean (was that really a surprise?) and two tourists with digital cameras, waiting patiently to see *Law & Order* start filming at the courthouse.

Sean was close to her, knees touching in the crowded space, but it wasn't the usual urgent touching that made her blood hum. This was different. This was…comfortable. They'd never had comfortable before. "So," he asked, "this civics streak inside you, is this new? Or have you always dreamed of running New York City?"

"I thought about being a ballerina," she answered, the coffee warming her insides. His eyes warming her skin.

"Really?"

"No, I was joking. I never wanted that. I wanted to be mayor. Actually, my first-grade goal was to be President, but my mother told me that I'd be better off as mayor. She told me that I'd make a great mayor."

Rachel Hollings had been a huge believer in giving back to the city, doing all sorts of little things that were never going to get a mention in the *Times,* but still set an example for Cleo to follow. Cleo, being Cleo, had magnified it forty-seven million times and made it her own. Thus, City Hall.

"You gonna run for mayor someday?"

She shrugged, not denying it. Someday held all sorts of possibilities for her. "Maybe."

"You should." She felt her insides warm even more.

"Why're you a lawyer?" she asked, wanting to know.

"I'm an excellent talker. Very persuasive."

"True," she admitted, watching him over the rim of her mug. "You always wanted to go into law?"

"Not always. I wanted to be rich. I don't like being poor, and I like the law. It seemed a good decision."

"And now? You ever second-guess yourself?"

"Never. No point."

"Nah, guess not. What are your brothers like?"

"You think the bar will be open today?" he asked, trading one question for another, which she had noticed.

"Tonight he'll be open for business."

"Come with me, then. Meet them. I'll get you home early," he said before she could protest.

"Maybe. Tell me about your brothers. Do you guys

fight?" His attitude was odd to Cleo because aggression was a job requirement for her. She'd learned it, mastered it. Sean seemed to actually like it.

"You don't have any brothers or sisters, do you?"

"No. Why, is that obvious?"

"Siblings fight. Fighting is an expression of love in our family."

"Sounds healthy," she said, trying to keep the sarcasm from her voice.

"Not," he replied, not missing it.

"Do you ever miss them? I mean, sometimes after you're used to them being around, and one day, you have to leave them behind, don't you miss them?" Her family had always been small and close-knit. First a trio, then a duo, and now Cleo was worried what would happen when it was only her.

"Of course I miss them. I have friends, but they're not family. It's not the same. The three of us shared a room for fifteen years. It was a total pain in the ass, but you do get used to having someone around. Daniel is a couple of years older than me, so he had two years alone, and then Gabe was alone for a long time after I went to school, but I always liked having somebody around late at night to talk to. We used to cut up and tease each other, and I miss that."

"And thus the midnight phone calls?" she asked with a smile.

"Yeah."

"I don't mind."

"I'm glad. Did you grow up in New York?"

"Born, raised, Rutgers is as far away from home as I get."

"A city girl."

"You betcha sweet ass, I am," she answered in her best Bronx accent.

"Bronx?"

"West Side."

"Really?"

"Same town house nearly all my life." She was flirting with the truth here, dropping little hints like bread crumbs to see if he would follow.

"Still there?" he asked, still following.

Carefully, cautiously, she nodded.

"Interesting," he murmured, but didn't press her anymore.

"What about you?"

"The Bronx, until my mother couldn't take it anymore, and made my father move, and then the Lower East Side, long before it was cool."

"Are your parents still around?"

Sean frowned, looked down at his cup. "No. Dad died nearly twenty years ago, and Mom died right after 9/11."

"That was a hard time." She remembered the endless days, sleepwalking through work and the deafening boom that would echo in her head at the oddest times. Still, her losses were nothing compared to others.

"Did you work it?"

"Not at the site, but we were all hands-on. Those were my public housing years, so I worked with the Red Cross on transitional housing for people who'd been displaced from the area."

"Daniel lost his first wife there."

"Your older brother, right?"

He nodded once.

"I'm sorry."

"Me, too."

She raised her cup. "To better times."

He looked at her and nodded. "I'll drink to that."

They talked for another few minutes, before reluctantly Cleo checked her watch. Playtime was over, back to the real world. "I have to go. It's almost eight-thirty."

"Meet me tonight, Cleo. Just for a little bit."

Helplessly she nodded. "I can only stay for a few minutes."

He leaned across the table and kissed her, whisper soft, and this time, her lips lingered.

"I know," he told her. "We'll work it out."

10

THAT AFTERNOON, SEAN CLOSED the door to his office and pretended he was preparing for his trial. Instead, he spent two hours staring at a blue spot on his wall, trying to understand when a spark became a flame became a bonfire became the fourth ring of hell.

He loved her.

Dear God, this was a death sentence. No, this was worse than a death sentence.

He'd never felt anxiety before. Not when he was negotiating multi-million-dollar settlements nor showboating for the jury nor prepping for the bar exam nor even when he played Ohio State in the Rose Bowl on a cold January, and not even when he realized that the defensive lineman outweighed him by at least five thousand pounds.

Being in love with Cleo Hollings was what sent sweat pouring down his neck, and caused his stomach to tighten into a Gordian knot.

What if she was married? Or what if she had a kid? Honestly, a kid didn't bother him. Or what if she couldn't love him? What if the rumors were true, and Cleo didn't have a heart?

Oh, man, this was worse than hell.

His cell phone rang, and it was Joe, the P.I. that Sean had hired a few days ago.

"You wanted to know about Cleo Hollings."

No. He didn't want to know. For the first time in his life, Sean preferred to live in the dark. However, that couldn't last, so he put down his pen and closed his eyes. "Yeah."

"She lives over on the Upper West Side with her mother. Converted town house. They live on the top floor. No kid. No pet. No husband. Her uncle lives in an apartment below them, and manages the rest of the apartments in the building."

"Her mother?" Sean repeated stupidly.

"Yeah. Rachel Hollings is sixty-three, married twenty years, until her husband died. Did some work as a secretary for some time, but stopped after her daughter was born. Cleo was an only child. Received a BBA from Rutgers. Lived in New York for two years, then her official residence, according to the DMV, became her mother's apartment."

Her mother. "Do you know if her mother's disabled?"

"That I don't. Probably something like that. Seven years ago, the mother's credit history came to a stand-still. Want me to find out?"

"Yeah. Find out everything you can," answered Sean and hung up.

Her mother?

Cleo was taking care of her mother.

It took a moment for that image to sink into his brain because it didn't fit. Cleo would outsource. She wasn't the soft type. Or was she?

That would be a huge responsibility. Okay, yes, it was smaller than running New York City, but still a time-consuming task.

A task that consumed all her time.

Cleo Hollings?

Okay, he processed the information, slowly easing into this new reality. As life-changing circumstances went, it really wasn't that strange. People took care of their relatives all the time.

But Cleo? Wicked Witch of Murray Street, Cleo?

Sean, that question has been asked and answered. Move along. Yes, she was taking care of her mother. Yes, there was a part of her that she kept from everyone—including him—but he understood why she kept it from the mayor. Hell, Sean kept all his pro bono work from Bruce, too. So what?

But *Cleo?*

He remembered her eyes this morning, that one second, that one look that had seared right through him. One look that had scared him completely.

It still scared him because that look belonged to a woman who was fragile and vulnerable, a woman who could get trampled on by a man who was emotionally stunted. Like, for instance, Sean.

Objection. Counsel was badgering himself.

This was a problem worth long, thoughtful consideration. He knew she didn't trust him, at least not with her secrets. Some people would construe that lack of trust to be a roadblock.

He picked up his pen and started to write, since he had no idea how to carry out an actual relationship, he thought he should develop a relationship strategy. After fifteen minutes of anxious finger drumming and staring at a blank yellow legal pad, Sean decided that strategy was probably overreaching. Better to start out with a simple tactical plan.

Step one. Tell her I know about her mother.

Better to just put the truth out there, let her yell, possibly hit him and get the roadblock out of the way.

Tonight. He'd tell her he knew tonight. Assuming she didn't call and cancel on him first.

Step two.

What went into step two? Would she even talk to him after step one, after she realized that he'd had her investigated? Probably not. Without talking, step two became even more difficult, so Sean scratched it out.

After further consideration, the apocalypse probably would have been easier.

IT WAS SIX O'CLOCK when Cleo got to the bar, and it was already packed. Swimming with men, and lots and lots and lots of women.

Why was she surprised? She stood in the doorway of Prime, her eyes searching the crowd, finding Sean instantly. He was laughing, smiling, having a grand old time. His eyes met hers, he stopped laughing, stopped smiling and moved through the crowd, like a shark smelling blood.

Anticipation shot through her because he was about to touch her. If anyone looked, they would know they were lovers, the air popping with it, but no one noticed except for her. Time slowed, the whetted throb of her blood running through her veins, firing her nerves, settling between her thighs.

His strong hands moved to her face, holding her there, and she saw the tantalizing expectation in his eyes. One thumb moved over her cheek, and if she were an infatuated woman, she would call it a caress. He was about to kiss her, and like an infatuated woman, her eyes drifted closed. Waiting for the touch of his mouth.

His hands fell away.

He was supposed to have kissed her. Why didn't her kiss her?

"I can't stay long," she said, wishing he would use his persuasive mouth to coax her into staying.

"I know," he said, not arguing, not trying to change her mind, and she wondered if it was smart to duck out after only an hour, leaving Sean with, roughly, thirty unscrupulous females most of whom were blond. "I want to talk to you about something before you leave."

"What?" she asked curious, and right then a blond approached, tugged at his sleeve like a four-year-old, and Cleo tried to look confidently amused, anything but jealous.

"Sean," the blonde said, kissing his cheek. Cleo's eyes narrowed.

Sean coughed. "Cleo, this is…." He looked at the blond and frowned.

"Tiffany," she said, still smiling, as if Sean's polygamous nature didn't bother her at all.

Cleo's frown grew darker.

Tiffany looked at Cleo, got scared (Cleo did that to people sometimes) and promptly fled.

"So this is what the bar looks like with people in it? Very nice." There were four bartenders working, three waitresses moving slowly through the crowd, and everywhere people were drinking. Wine, beer, cute little drinks with cherries in them.

"You want something to drink?" he asked. "Scotch, wine, screaming orgasm with a twist?" The words were meant to be meaningless teasing, the usual lines, but the mouth wasn't cooperating. He was trying to joke, keep things light, but something had changed.

"You are a card. Scotch. Neat."

He reached out to touch her hand, but then he stopped. "After you," he said, gesturing toward the bar.

"It looks very crowded for six o'clock on Friday," she said, as she followed him into the mass of teeming bodies.

"It's a party."

"You know all these people?" she asked. Her circle of acquaintances was huge, her circle of friends was now nonexistent. Her friends had gotten tired of Cleo saying "no," and after a while, they stopped asking.

"A lot of them. The old codgers sitting at the bar have been coming in for nearly forty years. That's Gabe behind the bar and Daniel's hiding downstairs. The bossy woman sitting at the back bar is Tessa. She's with Gabe. And the blonde next to her is Catherine. She's with Daniel."

"And the other thirty women?"

"Not a clue."

"Sean!" one of the other thirty women yelled.

Cleo tried to look urbanely amused. "I expected your talents for deception to be higher."

"I object. You work for a politician, and by the very incestuous nature of your appointment, some people would consider you to be a politician as well, and yet I have ascribed none of the slanderous labels often, *often,* associated with the politicians in this city to you."

"A credible defense, counselor. I apologize."

"You don't have to apologize if you were jealous."

"I'm not jealous," she said, watching one of the blondes brushing past him.

"Okay."

"I'm really not. I mean, puh-lease. How many of those women are Deputy Mayor? None. Jealous? I don't think so."

"You don't have any reason to be. Honestly."

"I'm not."

"Okay." He repeated, in a way that indicated he thought she was, which ticked her off.

"What did you want to talk about?" she asked.

"It can wait," he stalled, which fired her curiosity, because Sean was not a staller, not even remotely a staller. "Why don't you sit at the back bar with Tessa? Gabe would pay you big money if you could convince her to marry him."

He shouldered his way past four more friendly blondes, and led her to a vacant four inches against the bar.

"Want to meet Gabe? Gabe!" he yelled, assuming that she would fall completely in line with his wishes.

Cleo frowned, but then the bartender appeared who looked kind of like Sean, but…nicer, not quite so… tough. "Gabe, this is Cleo Hollings. She's the one who got your bar opened. You need to thank her."

Gabe smiled, a nice, friendly smile at her, completely without malice. "I owe you hugely for whatever you've done. And assuming that my brother hasn't already seduced you into willing compliance, whenever you want to come in and drink—it's on the house."

In other circumstances, Cleo wouldn't have been that bothered, but given the groupielike atmosphere (okay, that was a little melodramatic, but all the women *were* friendly) Cleo wasn't going to take the remark lightly. She gave Gabe a cold smile, and his face froze.

"You know that was a joke, right? Not an insult? Sean, explain that was a joke, will you?"

Sean looked at Gabe. "Pour out two Scotches, neat, while I use my lawyer words and we'll both hope it works." Then he turned to Cleo. "Yes, that was a joke. A few poorly constructed words designed to tease his brother, and in certain cases, it is possible that such words may unintentionally cause emotional or social injury, known or unknown to any person or persons, and should not be taken as slanderous, nor considered to be defaming of character in any way." He took a deep breath and then looked at her slyly. "I mean, really, seducing you into willing compliance? It wouldn't be possible, would it? I should tell you that I am willing to try."

"I don't think that's possible," she said, looking him over, keeping the lust out of her eyes.

His mouth inched up at the corner. "I know that look. I know what it means, and somehow, someday, somewhere, we're going to test that theory."

"But not now," she stated, thinking about it, wishing it wasn't possible, but she was afraid that boat had already sailed.

"Fine. Spoil my fun," he said, as Gabe pushed the two drinks down the bar with practiced ease. He introduced her to the two women sitting at the bar. Tessa and Catherine.

Tessa was short and tiny with sharp-cut brown hair and a gaze that never rested far from Gabe. She was easy to peg. It was the other woman that wasn't so easy to read. Catherine was taller, taller than Cleo, with watchful brown eyes and ash-blond hair pulled back from her face. It was obvious that she didn't feel nearly as comfortable in the bar as Tessa.

"Sean!" At least this time it wasn't a hot blonde. Gabe was yelling. "Help. Please."

Sean stood, took off his jacket, handed it to Cleo and rolled up his sleeves. "I think he's swamped. Give me a minute."

As soon as he left, Tessa didn't mince words. "You aren't married, are you? Gabe thinks you're married."

Cleo shook her head. "Not married."

She nodded once. "Good."

Catherine leaned forward, peering above Tessa's head. "I didn't think you were married. I thought it was just Sean."

"What does 'just Sean' mean?" asked Cleo, curious.

Catherine stopped. "He doesn't handle confusion well. You confused him. He didn't know what to think."

Cleo considered that, decided that it was close enough without explaining the whole mess of their relationship.

"I'm cautious with men," she told them, honestly.

Tessa nodded. "Me, too. I had Denny tattooed on my butt. Nothing like a mistake in permanent ink to inspire caution."

"Denny? Mine was Danny. But I never got tattooed. You really did that?"

"Took it off three years ago."

"Wow. You know, I think I feel better about it now. Thank you."

"What did Danny do?" asked Catherine, peeking around Tessa.

"You know how you think the best about someone, and it's completely not true, and you realize that they're actually lower than East River scum, and you've misjudged them completely only because you were infatuated with the idea of them?" It was a careful response, a vaguely political response, yet still a true response.

"Completely," replied Tessa. "He cheated on you, didn't he?"

Cleo considered that one for a minute. "No. I guess he wasn't lower than East River scum. I just wanted to think that. But he wasn't the guy I wanted him to be."

"I could get a tattoo," said Catherine. "Something very Renaissance."

"As long as it's not a man's name," warned Tessa.

"Is that why you don't want to get married?"

Tessa scowled, looking not nearly so friendly. "You're not supposed to know all this. How do you know all this?"

"Sean told me," admitted Cleo.

"He talks to you about his family?" Tessa asked.

"He didn't say anything about Daniel, did he?" asked Catherine.

"No fears. He doesn't say that much." Cleo looked at Tessa and smiled. "He likes you, and he thinks it's kind of…" Cleo stopped, realizing the Scotch had loosened her tongue, and now Tessa was staring at her with insane curiosity, in the way of people who find that their personal life has been discussed in great detail behind their back.

"What?"

Cleo exhaled. She should have kept her mouth shut. "Silly," she finished.

"Silly? Really? I don't think it's silly. Getting married is a very serious decision."

"You're terrified, Tessa," said Catherine. "I mean, we all know that."

"I could get a Gabe tattoo," whispered Tessa.

"Why would you do that?" asked Cleo, because there was a softness in Tessa's eyes, and it wasn't hard to figure out that she was nuts for Gabe, and if she was willing to do her worst for him, then why not give him what he wanted? Sean was right. It was silly.

"I think he'd like it better if you married him instead."

"Do you want to know why? I moved in with Denny at eighteen. Stupid mistake number one. I decided to forgo college and career because I thought he would take care of me. Stupid mistake number two. He did not take care of me, so I moved to New York. Stupid mistake number three."

"Mistakes aren't that awful, Tessa. And you were young. And besides that, now you have a solid career, a great apartment and Gabe. If you hadn't made those mistakes, you wouldn't be here now."

"Right," said Cleo, because it sounded good. "You should just flip a coin. Take all the decision making out of it."

"Flip a coin and decide if I get married?"

"Sure," said Cleo, handing her a quarter.

"I should do this?"

Cleo nodded. Tessa looked at Catherine. Catherine didn't look as convinced as Cleo, but she nodded.

"You have to decide what's what before you flip it," said Cleo, because rules were important in this game.

"Heads, I marry him. Tails, I don't."

The coin spun up, a flash of silver, Tessa plucked it in midair, and then plunked it down on her arm. "I don't want to look."

"Lift up your hand, and I'll look."

Cleo looked. Saw heads. "It's tails," she lied. "Sorry."

Tessa's face fell. "Really? I was hoping it was heads."

"Then you want to marry him," declared Cleo, because to her and apparently everyone else, it seemed obvious. "So marry him."

"I should, shouldn't I?"

"Do you think *this* is a mistake?" asked Catherine, and slowly Tessa shook her head.

Cleo held up her hands. "There you go. And by the way. It's heads."

"You don't ever make a mistake, do you?" Tessa looked at Cleo with hero worship in her eyes. Misplaced hero worship, but Cleo wouldn't be Cleo if she wasn't insanely flattered.

"I had a Danny. Not a Denny. Same story, same characters. Foolish girl who trusts a guy. Gets dumped. Realizes that said dumper was a total jerkola and kept hitting myself on the head for being so blind to reality."

"But no tattoo?"

"No. Didn't do that. Career stuff is not a problem. Personal stuff? That's an epic disaster." Cleo shrugged, dismissing the past.

"But Sean likes you."

"Sean likes all women."

"No, Sean loves all women. He likes you."

"Maybe," said Cleo. Sean saw her watching him, and came across.

"You okay? I'm sorry about deserting you. Duty calls," he said.

"It's all right. What did you want to tell me?"

For a second, he hesitated, but then he glanced at Tessa and Catherine, and pulled Cleo aside. "I know about your mother."

"What about my mother?" asked Cleo, not about to be trapped into admitting something that he didn't know merely because he was good at finding out what he wanted.

"I know you take care of her."

"Well, duh. Doesn't everybody."

"I know she's sick, Cleo."

"How do you know?" Although it wasn't a state secret, there was no way for Sean to figure this out. Cleo kept things well under wraps.

"I just do," he answered, dodging the question.

"How, Sean?"

"Don't make me tell you this. You're going to be mad."

"I'm not going to be mad."

"You'll be mad."

"Tell me."

"Private investigator."

Cleo stopped cold. Out of all the ways Cleo had envisioned for Sean to find out, this wasn't the one that she entertained. "You had me investigated?"

"I thought you were married. You knew that. And you weren't going to tell me."

"I would have told you."

"After how many years, Cleo?"

She ignored that, staring at his face, not surprised by the hard ruthlessness there. It didn't scare her. Didn't shock her. She didn't even fault him for hiring the P.I. Yeah, it tweaked a little, but honestly, this was a much easier battle to fight than the other one. The one about her mother.

"I can't believe you had me investigated. It's so…cold."

"You didn't give me a choice. I wasn't going to trust you until I knew why you wanted me to trust you."

"We were having an affair, Sean. Nothing more."

"That's such crap. You know it."

"I've only known you a week."

"So?"

"So, you want me to tell you this that fast?"

"Yes, I do. I don't sit around and wait, Cleo. I never have. I never will. You don't, either. It's why you're who you are, it's why you're where you are, it's why you're with me."

It all sounded so simple to Sean, so neat and tidy and easy. "You don't understand." He didn't have the pain of watching someone you love slowly vanish, the long nights, the hard slog of knowing that there was another person in the world that you couldn't let down. Ever.

"You're right, Cleo, I don't. Unless you tell me, I won't."

"Sean," she started, and then realized that she wasn't going to do this. Not here. Not surrounded by large clumps of happy people drinking and celebrating life. "We'll talk about this later."

"Don't be mad, Cleo. It's going to be okay."

"No, it's not. It's not going to be okay. It's hell, Sean, and most people aren't comfortable living there."

He looked toward the door and swore.

"What?"

"I didn't want to deal with this now."

"What?" she repeated, eager for another diversion. Cleo was an expert at stalling when necessary.

"Some guys from college are here. What time do you have to be home?"

"If I'm home by nine, it's good. Mom usually stays up until eleven, unless it's a bad day." *There,* she told herself proudly. She told him the facts without dressing it up nicely. If he didn't want to be sheltered from this, then okay, she wasn't going to shelter him. Besides, the sooner he understood what he was getting into, the faster he would run. She didn't want to analyze the pain that that caused. Maybe later. Maybe never.

His hand pulled tight on hers, leading her toward the group near the door, performing odd introductions, a little proud, a little belligerent, a little…vulnerable.

There were four men, Pete, Jacob, Cole and Dylan, who apparently knew Sean well. They were all well dressed, all confident and cocky, and they all did the whole male hitting-slapping thing.

The one known as Cole spoke first. He had a practiced smile. "Sean, your taste in women has improved."

Sean made a kill motion at this throat.

Cleo looked at Cole, striving to be the peacemaker. "That's all right. I'm sure it has."

Cole, Jacob and Dylan were having a great time; Sean stood alone; and Pete looked massively uncomfortable. She had seen that look before, especially at the council meetings when one of the members was being voted against, fifty to one, and the one member didn't know where he belonged.

However, Sean didn't stand around for long. "Gentlemen, you look thirsty. Can I get you something?" Sean played the host well, finding a table for them, taking orders and going to get drinks, as if eager to escape.

"Are they always this lively?" she whispered to Pete. She'd seen several sides to Sean, but this one was new, and she couldn't figure out what was going on. There were undercurrents. Strange undercurrents.

"Usually. I don't see Jacob or Dylan. They live in Philly. Cole lives here."

Interesting, she thought, when Sean returned with the drinks, seating himself next to her. She was curious about who Sean considered a friend, who he considered an acquaintance and who he considered merely a means to an end.

Cleo didn't fault him for it, but she watched him with the other men, studied the flatness in his eyes and the polite laughter at their jokes. With each second, she could feel the tension escalating inside him, see the line of his jaw grow harder.

Sean saw her looking and slid an arm around her shoulders. Subtle and possessive. With his friends, he was laughing a little too loudly, and it wasn't because of the Scotch. That, he had barely touched, only because he was too busy touching her. The movements were small and subtle, and completely on purpose because Dylan was tracking Sean's hand with his eyes.

The conversation drifted from the past to careers, and Dylan asked Cleo what she did.

"Deputy mayor."

"Where?" he asked.

"New York," she replied, not liking the way Sean was smiling at Dylan. Possessive, proud and mean.

"You've got another winner," Dylan said, and Sean flushed, his hand falling away.

"Go to hell, Dylan," Sean said coldly, but this wasn't temper. This was something else, and she was surprised to see Sean being played. And he was being played. Dylan was subtle, manipulative, pushing, tweaking, hitting all the right spots.

"Oh, come on, Sean. I was being nice. This one isn't going to win a dogfight."

Cleo had known a lot of politicians like Dylan. She didn't like any of them, and if somebody thought she was going to let a pinhead mess with Sean, they'd be wrong. Seriously wrong, and Cleo decided it was time to step into the ring. "I don't think women need to be judged on their looks."

"Apparently your boyfriend does."

Sean leaned forward, and Cleo grabbed his knee, pressing it hard with two fingers. "Why don't you just say what you're dying to say, rather than dancing around it like an idiot?"

"Did he tell you about the time he won the dogfight contest at the frat house?"

Cleo smiled tightly. "No, I must have slept through the whole discussion on stupid college mistakes."

"He didn't think it was stupid at the time. He was proud of what he'd done."

"Shut up, Dylan," Sean snapped, his voice no longer cold. He was furious and not thinking.

Cleo stared down at Dylan. "You have issues with Sean, don't you? Why?"

She had her own guesses about what Dylan's issues were, but she was curious about what he'd say, and she noticed how Jacob and Cole were watching Dylan with reserve. Group dynamics were a powerful tool that were easily exploited. Find the weakness, poke at it with a stick until somebody did something stupid, usually within record time.

"I don't have issues," Dylan argued, his tone defensive.

"Jacob, does Dylan have issues?"

Jacob nodded, and Cleo looked at Dylan, not hiding her scorn. "It bugs you, doesn't it? The high-class lawyer from the wrong part of town that gets all the girls. Got bit by the green-eyed monster, didn't you?"

"You're a total bitch, you know that?"

Sean half rose, and Cleo jabbed her fingers into his knee again, making him sit down. She could handle this. She could handle this toady with one hand tied behind her back.

Cleo leaned forward and smiled at him. "You have no idea. I could have forty cops in here hounding your ass and arresting you for whatever strikes my fancy. I could have your car permanently impounded within the city limits. I could kill off whatever corporate sales you *ever* wanted to make in Manhattan with a phone call. Yeah, I'm a total bitch, Dylan, but it's worse. I'm the total bitch with *all* the power in this town, and you really, *really* don't want to make me mad."

His face paled under the winter tan, and he stood. "I'm leaving." He looked expectantly at Jacob and Cole, who were both staring at the floor. That was the way of wars. People picked sides. Winners. Losers. And the losing side was never the one they wanted to be on.

Dylan threw his jacket around his shoulders in a diva-worthy gesture and stormed out.

Cleo leaned back in her chair. Yep, she still had it.

Sean looked at her, and she could read the surprise

in his face. He obviously hadn't expected her to defend him, but Cleo fought hard for the people she…liked. She blinked a couple of times. She was tired, she was cranky, and yes, she still hadn't forgotten that he had hired a detective to investigate her.

Cleo had one reason and one reason only for beating up on someone who was attacking Sean. Target practice. Nothing more.

"You didn't think they called me the Wicked Witch of Murray Street for nothing, did you?"

Jacob looked fascinated. "Would you really have had him arrested?"

Sean laughed. "Yeah. She would."

Cleo glanced at Sean, and wished he didn't have those dark take-no-prisoners eyes that never failed to stir her. She blinked back the haze.

Target practice.

Nothing more.

THE BAR ONLY GOT LOUDER as the evening crowd started to pile in, but Cleo was quiet. Too quiet. Sean looked at her, more than a little nervous, but before he started the conversation he dreaded, he started off a conversation that was more interesting. "Why did you do that?"

Cleo shrugged. "I was showing off."

Silently, he waited for the other shoe to drop. He waited for her to zoom into the fray, accuse him of hurting the innocents of the world, putting ugly women in a contest against their knowledge. Accuse Sean of being chauvinistic and a subversive misogynist or any of those other "ists" that he was sure she secretly thought about him, none complimentary. This time, he deserved it.

"Doesn't it bother you? Don't you want to know?"

Sean figured that Cleo would have jumped all over the dogfight incident like a cat jumping on a wounded canary.

"About what happened in college?"

"Yes."

"You want to tell me about it?"

Ah, he'd rather have a root canal, although he met her eyes, noticed the wariness there. "Not really, but I will. It wasn't my most shining moment."

"Didn't think it was. What happened to the girl?"

"Marnie never spoke to me again, went on to marry the Einsteinian chemistry major and last Paul told me they now have four highly intelligent children."

"So she survived," she said flatly, and he wished he could read her mind, wished he could tell what thoughts were going on in her head, but he didn't have a clue, and she wasn't helping. Cleo's opinion mattered a lot to him.

"I think so." Over the years, he'd debated the right way to handle things. At first, he'd called. Got hung up on. Then he wrote. Letters were returned. Eventually, he stopped trying to repair the damage, but that didn't make it easy to live with.

"Why'd you do it?"

Sean frowned. "Pride. I was tired of Dylan's putdowns. I wanted to win."

"You'll have to live with it. I think you'll do fine," she said, then downed the last drops of her Scotch and picked up her coat. "I need to go."

Sean stood, feeling deserted, not wanting to feel deserted and wondering if he was supposed to be feeling deserted. "Cleo?"

"I'll talk to you later," she said, and then headed for the door.

11

CLEO SENT HER DRIVER HOME. She needed to walk, she needed to move, she needed to think.

What was happening to her?

She walked from Tenth to the river, following the path north, the gravel crunching under her feet. The water was black in the moonlight, a few barges chugging along, a few dedicated joggers running by, running past the stupid lady who had thought she was smart and above all the other stupid women who had a Danny skeleton in her closet. She'd made her mistake, learned from it, never to repeat it again. So why did she feel as if she was repeating it again?

He was incredibly talented. Ruthless. Vulnerable. Proud. Humble. Hard. Gentle. She believed him. She believed in him. She trusted him. She didn't want to, she knew this was wrong, but she did. Tonight she'd been confronted with things, not once, but twice. Dylan had talked about the girl that Sean had humiliated but all Cleo could think of was a thousand excuses for him. Sean had hired a P.I. to go behind her back and find out about her life, and it didn't even faze her that her privacy had been violated. The old Cleo would have raged like a banshee. This new, more malleable Cleo didn't even blink twice.

Sean was like that. People defended him. The wind

blew through her hair, and she pulled the coat tighter. She was cold, shivering and she smelled liked Sean. She hadn't even touched him, but she'd absorbed little bits of him into her skin, into her mind, into her heart.

No.

The alarm on her watch buzzed, reminding her that she was late. Reminding her of exactly what sort of issues she had with Sean. He made her forget her responsibilities, and she wouldn't let *him* do that. Wouldn't let anyone do that.

She stopped, and sensibly walked back to Twelfth street, when a motorcycle pulled up next to her.

Speak of the devil.

Sean pulled off his helmet, his eyes hard. "Tell me something. Why are you walking home alone? Where's your driver?"

"I sent him home."

"You run the transportation in this city. Can't you use it?"

"I felt like walking."

"Can I give you a ride?"

"That's okay. I'd prefer to walk." She didn't want to be near him at the moment. If she rode with him, next to him where she could touch him, it would only make things worse. Right now, she had responsibilities at home, and she needed the mind-clearing distance.

"If you don't get on, then I'll be forced to follow you there."

And he would. "The law says both of us have to have a helmet. Sorry."

"Cleo, you're Deputy Mayor. Have you fixed a parking ticket before?"

"This is a moving violation. That's different," she lied.

"Cleo," he warned. "*You* wear the helmet."

"Fine," she agreed, because when he was around, he could seduce her into willing compliance, all without seduction. Cleo climbed on behind him, wrapped her arms around all that hard warmth, and put the helmet on her head.

The cologne smell was there again. She sighed.

Great. Just great.

"Where to?" he asked, and she froze, because this was a lot more serious than smelling his cologne. He wanted to come to her apartment, meet her mother, see Cleo's life up close and personal.

No. She was in no condition for that. Not yet.

Cleo got off the bike, returning the helmet to him. "That's okay."

"Cleo. You don't have to invite me up," he said, exactly as if he knew what she was afraid of. "Give me the address and I'll drop you off. It's not a big deal. Don't make it a big deal. I'm only trying to help."

"You're sure?" she asked.

"I'm positive. Give me an address, and I'll walk you to the door. I might take a kiss, sue me. However, I should tell you that I'm a good lawyer, so it wouldn't be wise." He handed her back the helmet. "Here."

Reluctantly, very, very reluctantly, she climbed onto the bike, her skirt riding up dangerously high. Her arms slid around him like they wanted to stay there, and by the time they reached Eighty-first Street, her thighs were wrapped around him like they wanted to stay there, too.

He stopped in front of her building and helped her off the bike, and in spite of all the things that she had learned tonight, she wished he could stay.

"Thank you," she told him primly, and he walked her up the steps to the entrance.

"Could you get out for breakfast in the morning? Or I could pick up some bagels and coffee."

"I've got things to do," she told him, and she did. There were groceries to have delivered, bills to be paid, and in the afternoon, she would take her mother for a long walk.

"Someday," Sean told her, and then he kissed her.

Her eyes drifted closed, her mouth opened, this was so familiar to her, so warm, so easy, so simple. It was only a kiss, but his kisses were the most dangerous. His mouth was persuasive, a mouth designed to sway juries and women, and she clung to him. The toughest woman in New York, clinging as if she needed him.

The door opened, and she stopped her clinging. It was her uncle.

"Cleo? Sorry to interrupt, but we need you upstairs."

Sean maneuvered her into the interior hallway, where he looked at Elliott and smiled. "Hi. Sean O'Sullivan."

"Elliott Macguire, Cleo's uncle."

Cleo looked at Sean, then looked past the stairway toward the small elevator tucked behind them. She didn't want to leave Sean alone with her uncle, and she wasn't about to bring him upstairs.

"I'll see you later, Sean. Thank you. For everything." It sounded like a dismissal, which is what she intended.

Sean stood there, hands tucked into his pockets, watching her with steady eyes, undismissed. "I can help you, Cleo."

"Go home, Sean. I like my life the way it is," she told him, because she wasn't going to give in. It didn't matter how hard it was or how much time it took or what it cost her.

"I didn't ask you to change it. Can I call you tomorrow?"

She should tell him no. She should end this now.

The word was even on her lips, but so was the feel of his kiss. She had known that kiss was dangerous. "Call me on the cell. I'll be in and out."

SEAN WAS BEATING HIMSELF UP because he shouldn't have pushed. He should have waited. She would have come around.

When hell froze, of course.

Her uncle was watching him with sympathetic eyes. "You're a brave man."

Brave? Is that what it was? That sounded so noble. Sean had thought he was a closet masochistic. He shrugged. "Fools rush in where angels fear to tread. What can I say?"

"I wish she'd let you help her. We need it."

Sean debated the wisdom of having this discussion with her uncle. Cleo would be furious if she knew, but if the old man knew Cleo well, he wouldn't tell her, and Sean sure as hell wouldn't tell her, and wouldn't it feel excellent to talk to someone who knew the details and would understand Sean's burning desire to beat his head against the brick wall that was Cleo.

"Her mother is your sister?" he asked, and the man nodded once.

"I'm sorry to ask this, but what kind of shape is her mother in?"

Elliott replied, "Not good. I hate to see Rachel like this, but we're both getting up in years. On some days she's mobile, fairly lucid, but the past two years she's gone downhill. It's hard on me, hard on Cleo, but she doesn't want to quit, and I don't bring it up much."

Sean handed him a card. "Can I ask you something? I'm a lawyer. My hours aren't crazy. The courtroom shuts down at four. Judges, they work banker's hours.

Can you call me if you need help, or if she needs help? She'll be mad, but I'll take the blame and she'll get over it. I think. I hope."

"Mad is an understatement. She hasn't said anything about you. You care about her?"

Closet masochist that he was, Sean didn't even try to deny it. "More than she knows."

Elliott looked at Sean, and apparently he passed the test. "I'll be in touch."

SATURDAY WASN'T THE EASIEST of days. Her mother wasn't eating, which was a new development. Cleo baked sugar cookies, scrambled eggs, fried bacon and roasted a chicken, and her mother only looked at her plate, looked at Cleo and said firmly, unequivocally, "No."

"Isn't there something I can make?"

Her mother stared out the window. "We could go for a walk. It's a wonderful day for a walk."

"It's too cold, Mom."

"I'll wear a coat."

"It's twenty-eight degrees, Mom."

"I don't mind. When I was twelve, you, Elliott and I made snowmen in our pajamas. Do you remember that, Margaret?"

Cleo nodded, wondering why her mother could remember her sister but forget her only daughter. Everyone said it was because of the disease, not because of Cleo, which worked the first time and the second time and even the third time. But sometime after that, rational explanations ceased to matter. "I remember."

She tried getting her mother to watch television, she pulled out the crossword puzzle, but no matter how hard she tried, nothing worked. Once again, Cleo was helpless. Nothing was going to help, either, but then in the middle of the afternoon, Sean called.

"I'm downstairs with hot chocolate, coffee, some deli sandwiches, sushi, bagels with cream cheese, a couple of baskets of flowers, chocolates and some movies. I didn't know whether to go action/adventure, which really sounded like you, or a classic, so I brought a selection of both and a few other things. Is that enough to bribe my way upstairs, or do I need to go out and get some more? I can get more."

Weakly Cleo collapsed on the couch. "You didn't."

"I did. The more pertinent question is, will it work?"

Cleo glanced at her mother who was studying her curiously. If Sean wanted to kill his free time spending it with her and her mother, fine. "Come on up."

Shortly he was at the door, arms empty, eyes alight, as if he had all the free time in the world. She looked him up and down. "Was all that merely a ploy to get up here?"

He shook his head. "Oh, ye of little faith." Then he snapped his fingers. "I have always wanted to do this," he said and opened their door wider. The parade into the apartment began with a young kid bringing in sacks of deli sandwiches, an older woman laden with fragrant vases of a rainbow of flowers, another boy with a hefty pizza box that smelled like garlic and hot mozzarella, a tuxedoed sommelier type bearing four bottles of wine, a man with DVDs and a bucket of buttery-yellow popcorn, a girl bearing fruit and pastry trays and two burly moving company types carrying a couple of tables.

Eventually, the apartment was full to the brim, but apparently everyone was well briefed because they began to set up with lightning efficiency, white tablecloths whisked out to cover the tables, shiny silverware was unpacked next. The florist arranged the sprays of flowers in large crystal vases. The sommelier unpacked candle stems, lit them with a flourish and then presented the wine.

In less then ten minutes the apartment was transformed, and Rachel Hollings stood there, mouth slightly ajar. "I think we're having a party."

Cleo looked at her mother, looked at Sean and shook her head in disbelief.

"I think we are."

IT SHOULD HAVE COME AS NO surprise to anyone that Sean completely charmed her mother. Sean and her mother spent the evening watching movies, sipping on wine and nibbling at strawberries, and Cleo spent the evening watching Sean. It might have been below freezing outside, but inside the apartment she was toasty warm, light and happy. Every now and then, she met Sean's eyes, expecting to see him bored or exhausted, but he seemed perfectly happy to crack jokes that made her mother laugh and didn't mind listening to her mother's stories for five times running.

It was nearly one in the morning when her mother sighed and looked at Sean, regretfully. "I have to go home now," she told him, and Sean didn't correct her, merely took her hand and bowed.

"The pleasure was all mine, Mrs. Hollings."

Actually, the pleasure was all Cleo's, but she didn't correct him. She helped her mother dress for bed, and tucked her in, giving her a kiss on the forehead.

"Did you have a nice time, Mom?"

"He's a lovely man, Cleo. Do you think he'll come back tomorrow?"

It was a question that Cleo had no answer for. Today had been a once-in-a-lifetime gift, but the thing about once-in-a-lifetime gifts, they usually only occurred once in a lifetime. "Probably not, Mom."

"Maybe he will if you ask nicely. You know, sometimes you get gruff. Try and remember your manners and say please."

Cleo smiled. "I will. Swear."

SEAN WAS WAITING ON the couch when she came back in the living area, and she sat next to him, unaccountably shy. Cleo had spent most of her adult years doing favors for people, usually without thank-yous. It was all part of the regimented "take a favor, owe a favor" that permeated city government. No one had ever done anything even remotely close to something like this. No, this was her best day ever. Considering the myriad perks that came with her job, this was no small accomplishment.

"Thank you," she said. "I didn't know what to expect from you."

"Underpromise, overdeliver. Works great for juries, as well." His arm stretched across the couch, his fingers stroked her neck, part comfort, part seduction, all magic.

"My mother likes you," she told him, feeling her skin come alive under his touch.

"And you're surprised by that because?"

"Every woman loves you, doesn't he?" she asked, not completely kidding. How did women not love him?

"Guilty as charged."

"I thought you worked at Prime on Saturdays. All the brothers there, wasn't that what you said?"

He shrugged it off. "Gabe can handle it," he said easily.

"I'm glad he's willing to share," she said, looking at him doubtfully. She hadn't expected this from Sean. Not sacrifice. It warmed her, but made her feel guilty as well.

"He's a big boy. Don't worry about Gabe," he assured

her, his fingers kneading harder into her neck, relieving the knot of tension that had sat there for what seemed like years.

"I wish you could stay," she whispered.

"Someday," he told her, a promise in his eyes, and she leaned into him, meeting him halfway. His mouth covered hers, tasting like wine and strawberries, and her favorite taste in the world—Sean.

The sensation of his kiss was engraved in her memory, the slow tangle of his tongue, the taste of him, the soft drag of his teeth over her lip, the rich smell of him that never failed to make her want. When he raised his head, she was weak, waiting for more.

"I'll go," he said, and her body let out a cry of protest, but Cleo tamped it down. He rose and pulled her up from the couch.

At the door, he kissed her again, and she opened the door, but this time, she pulled him back for one last taste. And she knew that one last taste wasn't enough.

"Can you stay for a little bit?" she asked, knowing that she had a twin bed, and her mother was sleeping in the room next door, and feeling like the most embarrassed teenager in the world, but tonight had been too perfect. She didn't want it to end. Not yet. She wanted perfection to linger.

She wanted Sean to linger.

He looked at her carefully. "You're sure?"

"I have a twin bed, and it's very small, and we'll have to be very, very quiet."

He kissed her again. "I'll do my best not to make you scream."

"I don't scream."

"Darlin', don't challenge me," he said, and she smiled and led him by the hand to the room that she'd grown up in, the room where she'd spent every night alone, but not tonight.

The clothes were shed with soft whispers, her fingers tracing over him as he undressed. His mouth was much more brazen, tasting the curve of her shoulder, the crest of her breast, the inside of her palm, until she pulled him into her bed, into her arms and his body covered hers, skin to skin.

Sean was no still lover, his mouth feasting wherever it landed, his hands stroking, teasing a nipple to hardness, finding the heat between her thighs, and Cleo's sighs grew more extravagant with each passing moment. "I should have a bigger bed," she said, because he probably had a huge bed, and she probably should have replaced the rock-hard mattress five years ago, but she'd never had enough time.

"I love your bed," he whispered, his teeth nibbling at the lobe of her ear, and she could feel his engorged flesh against her, hot, thick and velvety hard, and she slid her thigh against him, hinting, tempting, and was rewarded with a groan.

"Take me, Sean," she urged.

He lifted his head, stroked her face. "We don't have to hurry."

"Please," she told him, and he must have read the worry in her eyes because he nodded and then filled her with a stroke. Cleo kept thinking that this was a dream. That she would wake up and find herself alone, not staring into the eyes of the most perfect man in the world, but it wasn't a dream. He took her mouth, kissing her, making her wish, making her want, making her moan. With each thrust, he buried himself deeper and deeper inside her, until they were no longer two distinct bodies, but one.

He was the other part of her.

Cleo moved her head restlessly, burying her face against his shoulder, trying to hide from glinting dark eyes that saw too much, but that was no escape. The smell of Sean, his cologne, his sex, filled her as completely as his body did. There was no escape.

Small aching sounds that came from low in her throat. Pleading. And she had to be quiet, but it was so hard, and she wanted to push him away, but that was impossible, her body wouldn't let her. Her mind wouldn't let her. Her heart wouldn't let her.

He filled her. Over and over. Until there was no part of her untouched, until he owned her completely.

Finally, finally, she stopped resisting, gave herself up to pleasure, to him. Her body matched his, angry because she didn't need this, fated because she had no choice. Cleo bit her lip, tasted blood and came hard and fast. Sean followed, his hands tight on her hips as his body shuddered.

He lifted his head, studied her, and she looked away. His fingers grasped her jaw, made her look there, made her see the promise in his eyes. Cleo had never been so afraid in her life…

And never been so desperate to believe.

12

SEAN LEFT AT 3:00 A.M., but Cleo didn't sleep after that. Her bed smelled too much like him, like his cologne, like his lovemaking, like the trampled remains of her old life. And she spent many giddy moments simply lying there, staring up at the ceiling and grinning at nothing in particular.

He had made no promises for tomorrow, and she didn't want to expect any promises to see him tomorrow, even though, secretly, she knew she would love him forever if he promised her a mere hour tomorrow. Frankly, she was going to love him forever even if he didn't promise her a mere hour tomorrow, but that would cement the deal.

Love.

Cleo Hollings was in love.

She had become one of the ten thousand million gazillion women who already loved Sean, but Cleo had room for hope. This wasn't an affair. This wasn't scratching an itch, and no man, not even the ruthlessly persuasive Sean O'Sullivan, spent ten hours, and God knows how much money, entertaining a woman who would probably forget he existed tomorrow.

Rachel Hollings—not Cleo, because Cleo would never forget him. Ever.

She couldn't know what tomorrow would bring, but

as she hugged her pillow close, inhaling deeply, her heart sent up a tiny prayer.

One hour. Only one hour with the two people she loved most in the world. And if that wish came true, she'd open up four new homeless shelters, two free clinics and fight for the sanitation department's three percent wage hike that she'd been fighting against.

Her wish nearly came true. Sean was there at noon in dark jeans and a brown sweater and bearing pink roses for her mother and a bouquet of edelweiss for her. He explained it with an apologetic shrug. "I didn't know your mom well enough to decide, but you..." He shot her a warm look. "Edelweiss. Definitely."

"Oh," murmured Rachel Hastings.

"What?" asked Cleo.

Her mother gave a knowing smile. "Do you know what edelweiss stands for?"

"Daring," Sean answered quickly.

"Noble purity," replied Cleo's mother.

"Courage," said Sean.

"The queen's flower," answered her mother.

Sean stopped there and shrugged. "It seemed appropriate."

To Cleo, it seemed perfect.

For exactly thirty-seven minutes, he worked with them on the Sunday crossword, even letting Cleo beat him to habeas corpus, which endeared him to her, nearly as much as the flowers.

Nearly.

A phone rang and Cleo automatically looked down at her cell, but it was Sean's.

"One sec," he said, excusing himself, and she didn't want to blatantly eavesdrop on the conversation, but she did overhear enough to realize that he was telling

Mrs. Ward from the West Side Ladies Botanical Preservation Group that he couldn't make the meeting today, but he could meet with her for a few minutes after court.

When he came back to sit down next to her, she stared at the crossword. He wasn't Danny, he wasn't close to Danny. She loved what Sean was doing for her, and she knew exactly how much he was giving up to be with her, and very few people understood the true cost associated with that, but Cleo did. She knew only too well.

A few minutes later his phone rang again. He excused himself, and this time the conversation was longer. His boss. When he returned, Cleo didn't stare at the crossword, she stared at him.

"That was work?"

He nodded. "Bruce is needy and anxious and all sorts of things. The trial starts tomorrow. He doesn't sleep well then."

"There must be a lot on the line?"

"It's only money," he dismissed.

"Are you a financial tycoon?" asked Cleo's mother, blinking curiously.

"No, ma'am. I'm a lawyer."

"That's a shame," murmured her mother. "I had high hopes for you being a tycoon."

"Mother," Cleo said, in her warning voice.

Sean laughed. "It's fine."

"Do you need to go?" asked Cleo.

"No," he said, and his phone rang again. This time he swore under his breath. "I have to go."

"It's all right," said Cleo, because she felt uncomfortable knowing he was giving something up for her.

"I'll talk to you later," he said, and he kissed Rachel Hollings's hand, and he took Cleo outside the door and kissed more than her hand.

"Thank you," Cleo told him, after he raised his head. "Thank you for everything."

He grinned, completely unaffected. "I'll let you think of creative ways to repay me," he told her, and then he set off, leaving her to mull over all the creative possibilities.

SEAN NORMALLY DIDN'T have bad weeks, but the next one was a disaster. The Davies trial started on Monday, and one of his witnesses developed the flu, so Sean spent late hours on Monday trying to find someone who could fill in. The mayor had left town for Albany, leaving Cleo in charge again, and her schedule was full from 7:00 a.m. until 9:00 p.m. every day. He didn't get to talk to her, didn't get to touch her, all that was left was ragged voice mails left in the wee hours of the morning.

It wasn't enough.

On Monday, she told him that plans for dinner had been axed. He left a message explaining the problems with his witness. Then Gabe called wanting him to bartend on Thursday, and he hadn't wanted to bartend on Thursday, but apparently Tessa had decided to accept his brother's proposal—finally. And although Sean was very happy with that, he needed to go over the plans for the park with the West Side Ladies Botanical Preservation Group, and for him to do both, he wouldn't be able to see Cleo, and he badly needed to see Cleo.

On Wednesday, she left him an explicit voice message, telling him in exact detail what she was planning on doing to him the next time she saw him, which normally wouldn't be cause for complaint, except that Bruce happened to be sitting in Sean's office when he retrieved said message, and the sound of her voice so fascinated Sean that he didn't slam down the phone like he should have. Instead, he sat there listening, his cock growing and growing, until it reached alarming proportions. Sean couldn't move for twenty minutes afterwards, listening to Bruce whine, all while he wanted to slam the door shut and ease some of the frustration that was boiling inside him.

On Thursday morning, they actually met for coffee, but Sean was dead on his feet, and Cleo had a wastewater meeting to prep for, so what should have been wonderful turned into a heated argument over whether or not New York City's recycling percentages were adequate for the next ten years. It was stupid, pointless and should not have involved name-calling, but names were called, and Sean went to court, grilling an insurance clerk with more malice than normal until finally the judge had asked him to ease up.

It wasn't pretty.

On Thursday evening, Cleo came back to her office and there was a red rose on her desk. No note, no message, nothing but the single flower. She locked the office door, then collapsed into her chair, so tired, so drained, and quietly put her head down on her desk, but it wasn't dreams that came this time, but tears.

Cleo didn't cry. Tears were for the weak, but this wasn't fair. All week she had listened to Sean, listening as each day his voice grew tighter and tighter with tension. Each day, she had told herself not to feel guilty, and each day she had felt guilty. Last night, she had stopped at Prime because she thought Sean would be there, she'd thought she'd surprise him, but Tessa was there working because Sean was working on Thursday night, rather than Wednesday, which normally would have been the brothers' poker night, except Sean had missed it because he had some work to do for a trial.

Family. Sean was missing out on his own family for her.

The guilt came again. Bigger and badder this time, pulling at her, eating at her and reminding her that yes, her life was yuck, and yes, now his life was becoming yuck by association.

It wasn't fair.

The tears dried eventually, and she checked the mirror, wishing her secretary a good evening. Sean called her on her cell shortly thereafter.

"How are you?" he asked. "Mad?"

"Thank you for the flower."

"I'm sorry for this morning."

"You were tired. I was tired. It happens," she told him, wanting to ease his mind.

"Not to me," he said. "What's on the agenda for tonight?"

Cleo closed her eyes. "A dinner with the council members from Queens. Easy stuff. Listen to their demands, and then stuff shrimp into your mouth before you can actually promise anything you can't deliver. You have to work at Prime?"

"I promised Gabe."

"You should sleep."

"Someday," he told her. "You should know that because of you Tessa finally accepted Gabe's proposal. Tonight they're celebrating. Gabe wanted to give me the details. He's happy. You made them both very happy."

Cleo managed to smile. "That's great. Tell them congratulations. I'll see you tomorrow," she said, wishing that tomorrow was today.

"Promise?" he asked.

"Promise," she said.

"Are you all right?"

"Yeah," she lied. "Just tired."

"Get some sleep tonight. And Cleo?"

"Yes?"

"You'll dream of me?"

"I promise."

CLEO'S STINT AS MAYOR ended in dramatic fashion, and not exactly the drama she was hoping for. She was called from the council members' dinner because there was a four-alarm fire in a twenty-seven-story Bronx apartment building, When the first alarm went out, she was automatically notified, but she stayed at the restaurant, listening to the updates from her driver. When the second and third alarms went out, she called her uncle, and told him she wasn't sure what time she would be home.

By the time the fourth alarm sounded, Cleo was in the car, going to the scene. According to the reports, four families were unaccounted for, and two firefighters were sent to the hospital in serious condition.

Mayor. Ha.

Sometimes being mayor sucked.

THE FIRE LASTED FOR FIFTEEN hours. Fifteen freaking hours before the missing families were accounted for, fifteen hours before the firefighters brought it under control just as the sun was starting to rise. It seemed pink through the heavy gray haze of smoke, ash flying in the air like confetti. Every few minutes, firefighters emerged from the structure, sucking in oxygen. While Cleo argued with the Red Cross, who wanted to send the families to a shelter way the hell out in Connecticut, she tried to stay calm. She impatiently explained to the woman on the phone why the residents needed to stay at a shelter closer to their home, watching as one of the firefighters ran out and was treated for eye injuries, the medics pouring water over smoke-fogged eyes.

Cleo had never been one of the calm ones. She flew off the handle, she yelled, she had a wicked tongue and, most of all, she couldn't handle standing there, watching, doing nothing. She was helpless, and she hated it. Hated. It.

"Keep them in the city," she snapped to the clueless secretary on the other end, and then hung up because for tonight she was the mayor.

The buses arrived and the residents boarded. They were kids in pajamas and old men in robes, clutching coats, blankets, leaving their homes for who knows how long. One little kid smiled up at her, that brave, "nothing is wrong" smile and Cleo smiled back at him, wishing that she were one of those touchy-feely people who could hold him close and tell him that she would make it right. The adults were smarter—they didn't have those smiles. Cleo handed everyone one of her cards and told them to use it whenever they needed. It was probably more effective than a hug, but she wished she had retained that bit of humanity nonetheless.

Engines idling, the buses stayed there until everyone was on board, hollow faces pressed against the window watching this place that had been their home. And Cleo stood, rigid, stiff and unmoving because she didn't know how to make this transition as easy and as comfortable as possible.

Transition. Somewhere in the dictionary *transition* was another word for *screwed.*

She held a press conference at 4:00 a.m., answering the questions she knew, deferring to the chief for most of them. And by the time she left, her clothes were gray, she'd lost all sense of smell, and she was supposed to be in her office in less than two hours. The buses were gone, the firefighters were packing up equipment, and only the shell of a ruined building remained. Yeah, everything was back under control, except for her. Silently, she climbed into her car and pressed her face against the window all the way home.

"Elliott?" she called quietly as she unlocked the door to her apartment.

"He went to sleep at hour seven. Roughly."

Sean.

In her clean and nonburned-out home, Cleo felt dirty and empty inside, and she didn't have the strength to keep him at arm's length, nor sadly, the will. "You shouldn't be here," she said, wiping her face and ending up with an ash-covered hand. "You have a trial in the morning, and your brother…oh, God, what happened to Gabe and Tessa? They were going to celebrate."

"They're fine," he said. "No big deal." He was lying. It was a huge deal. He shouldn't be here, he should be taking care of his family rather than taking care of hers.

Her mouth worked furiously because she was inches away from tears, and she wasn't going to cry.

"You look beat," he said, most likely the understatement of the year, and she nodded once.

It shouldn't seem so right that he was seated on that love seat in her mother's apartment, since Cleo had fought tooth and nail to keep that love seat and this apartment, and she knew this wasn't a battle she was winning, and Sean wasn't a man to fight on the losing side. Sadly, Cleo was on the losing side.

His eyes were so gentle, and she didn't want him to be gentle with her because her heart couldn't take the additional guilt.

"Why don't you lie down?" he asked. "All you need to do is rest. A few minutes. Thirty at the most. I'll wake you up. I promise."

She wanted to send him away, leave all that seductive gentleness, but what would she do without him? Now, she needed him like she needed to breathe. "Do you promise?"

He nodded, and she knew he was lying, but she lay down on the love seat anyway, her head in his lap. She sniffed once, which was as close to tears as she would ever get in the presence of another human being, and he stroked her hair, and she sniffed twice because he was making it very difficult. She would have sniffed three times when he put his lips against her hair, but thankfully she never knew.

Cleo Hollings, Deputy Mayor of New York City, was fast asleep.

FRIDAY MORNING CAME WAY too soon, and her mother gave up eating again. The doctor had told her this was a possibility that might occur. He suggested she consider transitioning her mother to facilitated care. Cleo told him to go to hell, which probably wasn't the best way to speak to the doctor; however, she was tired of people underestimating her abilities. When Sean called, she felt better, but she didn't mention this latest crisis. Sean was in the middle of a trial, and she wasn't going to dogpile all her issues onto him as well. She'd dogpiled enough for one week.

However, just when she thought things were looking up, Mrs. Catsoulis, the afternoon sitter, called.

"Your mother is missing."

Her heart stopped. "Define missing."

"I was in the kitchen, making lunch, and she must have slipped out without me hearing her. I've looked in the building, and your uncle is helping me, but Miss Hollings, I think it'd be best if you came home."

Missing. Cleo reminded herself that it wouldn't do any good to panic. She needed to stay in control. After two deep breaths, the panic disappeared.

"I'll be right there," she said, pulling on her coat, grabbing her bag and yelling at Belinda that she was in charge.

She ordered her driver to speed up on the West Side Highway, calling the Central Park police station and checking on the weather. They were above freezing. She knew the drill, she'd learned the steps, but even preparedness couldn't prevent cold sweat from soaking the collar of her blouse.

Her mother always went to the park. Frantically, she watched as the clouds rolled in, praying the rain would hold off for a just a bit longer.

She could find her. Force of will.

Last weekend, when Sean had come over, when the three of them spent the day talking and laughing, she had thought that maybe—*maybe*—things were working out. Her mother seemed happy, and no doubt about it, Cleo was happy, too. For the first time in way too long, she was happy. And now she felt as if, once again, the bottom had dropped out of her world.

Why now?

The park cops were waiting when she arrived, marvelous, in control, used to finding the lost things in the park. Kids, parents, purses. It was old hat to them. Not to Cleo. Frantically, she passed the reservoir, around the Great Lawn, nearly running over a tourist near the museum, and still there was no sign of her mother. The clouds grew darker, and Cleo forgot not to panic. Panic was there in huge, oxygen-thieving bulk. This was her fault. Everyone had told her. She should have listened.

She had made it almost to the ball fields when the cops called.

"We found her. She's at Tavern on the Green. Waiting for afternoon tea."

"I'll be right there." And ten minutes later, her blood pressure still not recovered, she came to pick up her mother.

"Mom?" she asked, brushing past the hostess to the ornate velvet seats in the mirror-lined hallway.

Her mother looked at her blankly. "Margaret?"

"It's Cleo. We need to go home, Mom," she said, grabbing her arm because she wanted her mother home. And safe. Away from rain and cars and bad people and all the things that she'd conjured in her head.

"After tea," her mother insisted, pulling her arm free.

"Mom, we can't have tea."

"Maybe you can't, but I certainly can."

"Mother!" Cleo snapped.

Her mother stopped arguing, stood frozen, her eyes welling with tears. All around them, people stared at the bad person who made the helpless old woman cry.

"Please, Mother," she whispered, and this time her mother gathered her purse and the driver helped them into the car.

"I'm sorry. I wasn't trying to upset you," her mother apologized, sounding like a child, and Cleo wondered when it had come to this. When the possible became the impossible, when force of will just didn't cut it and when she was making her own mother cry. It wasn't fair. She was Deputy Mayor of New York City. Sean had made her believe in miracles. Sadly, miracles were for the deluded.

Carefully, as if she was handling a piece of glass, she hugged her mother, comforting her. Cleo told her that everything would be all right, all while wondering how she could make it all right.

When she got home, it was after five, Mrs. Catsoulis took over and the mayor, not realizing Cleo's personal trauma, called.

"Where are you?"

"Got called away. I'll see you on Monday."

"I'm looking for the financial plan. Where'd you put it?"

Damn, damn, damn.

"I'll be back, Bobby. Give me a couple of hours and I'll have the revised one on your desk."

"That's my girl," he said, encouragingly, not sensing the death glare he was getting over the phone.

Of course, by the time she got back to City Hall, the rain had started to fall in great sheets, blocking visibility, and Cleo had the driver drop her off at Canal Street. She started to walk in the rain, great splashing steps that sent pedestrians scurrying around her. She probably looked like hell. She felt like hell. Mostly she felt like she'd let her mother down. Cleo had worked through 9/11, worked through three transit strikes, managed the '05 blackout and blizzard, but such a simple task…

She had failed.

It took her fifteen minutes to make the necessary modifications to the financial plan and plop it on Bobby's desk. He looked over her appearance with a quirked gray brow. "Slumming, Cleo?"

She snarled, which was enough, but when she got

back to her office, Sean was waiting for her, warm and dry, and she wanted to walk into the safety of his arms and never look up again.

He took in her wet hair and clinging dress. "You look miserable."

Her mouth worked, ready to go into long and drawn out detail of exactly how miserable her day had been, and Sean would listen, comfort her, take care of her and make everything seem better when it wasn't. It was that one damning detail that made her keep her mouth shut about her problems. "How did the trial go?" she asked instead.

"We're winning," he said, as if there was never a doubt, since that was Sean's world. Winning. "What happened?"

"It doesn't matter," she snapped. "I'm tired. I'm going home."

"Cleo, what happened? You have that look. Your mouth gets really pinched. I know that look. What's wrong?"

"Don't ask," she said, pleading with him now. His eyes were looking at her, so warm, so comfortable, so easy, and she wanted to walk straight over to Sean, but she needed to stay strong and stop the denial that had been hounding her for way too long.

"What happened with your mother?" he asked, obviously knowing that yes, city government she could handle, but her personal life—not so much.

"She went outside for a walk."

Sean, being Sean, instantly knew this wasn't a good thing.

"You can't do this to yourself anymore," he said, and Cleo sighed. For nearly three weeks, she'd been waiting for this. She knew the words were there, waiting to be said, and yes, when her confidence had been shot to hell and she wasn't sure if she could manage anything, he was going to slap her with this. Finally, Sean had switched sides, and her heart, that little chamber that she'd recently rediscovered, faded to black once again.

She came back with an appropriately canned response. "Don't tell me what I can't do. I can do this. I'll work harder and it'll be fine."

"Cleo, stop," he said gently, and Cleo had never felt so alone in her life. Pre-Sean she'd been alone, but she'd never been lonely, she was too busy, too in love with her life. Now, after-Sean, she knew what it was like to be a couple, to talk to someone, to tease someone, to whine to someone, to be in love with someone.

Now, "alone" hurt, and deep in her heart she knew she was destined to be alone.

Never one to show her wounds, Cleo glared, and she had a first-rate glare. Her eyes narrowed, gleaming with fury that would strike fear into a lesser man, but Sean wasn't a lesser man. So, when eye glaring wasn't enough, she used her words instead. She had a great talent with words, and because he hurt her, she could hurt him back. Well honed instincts told her exactly where to hit.

"I knew this was going to happen. I knew it. But you didn't say anything, so I thought okay, I misjudged you. But I didn't. You're still that same guy, aren't you? You've only been waiting. Waiting for the right time. You're still that same bastard. Throw a helpless lady out of her own home."

He stood there, taking it from her once again, and now she was yelling at him. Just like she had yelled at her mother. The two people in the world she loved most, and all she could do was yell at them.

Cleo stopped. "I'm sorry."

He sat down in her chair, pulled her into his lap, ignoring the fact that she was soaked and he was dry, and for a few golden seconds she sat there, letting him stroke her hair, feeling better, but knowing that absolutely nothing had changed.

"I can't do this," she whispered, the words abnormally loud in her head.

"You don't have to do this, Cleo. There are really great places for your mother. I know it's not what you want, but you're killing yourself."

He thought she was talking about her mother.

"I can't leave her alone, Sean. She won't survive without me."

On the other hand, I can survive without you. It won't be easy, and I'll miss you, but I will survive, and I'm not going to take you down with me.

His hand stilled because Sean must have figured it out. It was one of a million reasons that she loved him. Fingers slid down to her jaw and he tried to make her look him in the eyes. Stubbornly, her head stayed against his chest.

"You're giving this up? Quitting? Giving up on us?"

"It was fun," she told him, pretending that that's all it was.

"Oh, no, Cleo. If you're going to do this, you're going to look at me." There was a tone in his voice, and his fingers jerked at her jaw, forcing her to meet his eyes. For a moment, she could fake it. She could fake that this wasn't the hardest thing she'd done in her life, but he saw it for what it was. A sham.

"You think this is impossible, but it's not. I can help you."

"No," she said. "You've done too much already."

"I can do more," he said, echoing words that she'd said herself only a few days before. Yes, he could do more. Yes, she could do more. They could both work harder, work smarter, and in the end, it wouldn't be enough. Instead of one miserable person, now there'd be two.

She wouldn't let that happen.

"Sean, no. It's not going to work." Quickly she stood because she couldn't be touching him, couldn't be leaning into all that strength. The Wicked Witch of Murray Street was back. A little wiser. A little sadder and even tougher than before.

He rose, but he didn't touch her. "We're not done, Cleo. I know what you're doing, and I won't let you."

"You don't have a choice."

His smile was hard and a little bit mean. "I don't have a choice? No. I haven't even started to fight for you, Cleo. Just wait."

She rubbed her eyes because she couldn't fight him, and he was going to make her fight him. "Why can't you go away?"

He answered her question with another. "Why are you fighting so hard for your mother, Cleo?"

This was a trap, and he was leading her there by the nose, hooking her with his words. "Because I love her."

Sean nodded once. "Exactly."

13

CLEO SANK IN HER CHAIR after he left because when he fought dirty, he really, truly pulled out all the slings and arrows, the exact weapons guaranteed to decimate her.

He loved her.

How did a man fall in love after three weeks? It was too soon, she told herself.

Too soon for her to be in love, too?

No.

He would be miserable with her. She was mean and crabby and demanding and selfish.

He knew all that and loved her anyway.

That was the most lethal part of it.

Slowly, she pushed back her desk chair and went outside, ready to go home. What did it change? Anything? Not really.

Sean O'Sullivan loved her? Maybe he could work miracles. As she headed toward the street where her driver was waiting, the bitter wind cut through the drenched wool dress, but in spite of the cold, there was a tiny smile toying hopefully around her mouth.

"CLEO, I HOPE YOU'RE NOT sleeping well. I hope you're not eating. I'm not. I kept dreaming last night, and you were there with me, and I woke up alone, and I almost hated you for it. Almost.

"I've never loved a woman before. Honestly. There was a girl when I was in third grade, and she was cool, but I yelled at her one day and she ran off and cried to the teacher, and that was pretty much the end. In college, I had a couple of close calls, but I dodged them nicely, because I knew they weren't the One. Something was always missing. I was waiting for you. Do you ever feel that way? Like there're millions of others out there, but there's only one. My other half. You. Daniel always sported that drivel at a wedding, and I laughed at him for it. Someday I'll tell him he's right. I'll talk to you tomorrow.

"I love you."

LATE THAT NIGHT, when she was waiting for sleep, Cleo picked up the phone and punched in his number, listening to his voice mail. *He loved her.*

"Sean,

"You are the devil. I should hate you for making me weak, but I can't. I want to do everything. I have the best job in the world, I want to provide the best care ever for my mother, and I want to love you in the way you should be loved. I want all three, and you know, I'm pretty good at denial, but I think if I tried to tackle all that—that's a lot of denial—even for me. Last week, I hated what was happening to you. I hated that you couldn't be there when Gabe needed you. I hated that you stayed up all night prepping for a trial when you should have been able to sleep. I know about that lack of sleep thing. It's a killer, and I hated that you were paying the price for helping me. I'm not sure if you could see what was happening to you or not. Maybe you knew and didn't care, maybe you didn't notice, but I could see it. I was responsible. It sucks.

"I love you, Sean. You're right. I was wrong, but

what am I supposed to do? Even if I wanted to leave my job, I can't afford to. I won't abandon my mother. She needs me. She's not like you. She's not strong. I don't have her for very much longer, Sean. I want all the time that I have with her. There isn't a way out, and you're leading me right back into denial, and I don't think that's smart.

"I don't think you should leave me any more messages.

"Goodbye."

ON SUNDAY MORNING, he showed up at her door in black slacks, gray cashmere sweater and a heated flush in his eyes.

"You tell a man you love him in a voice mail?" he nearly yelled to the entire building.

Cleo took a discreet step out into the hall before her mother knew he was there. "You did it first," she felt the need to point out, wishing her nerves were calmer, and her pulse rate would control itself.

Sean exhaled deeply and held up a hand. "Cleo, I think we need to talk."

"We're talking now."

"Alone."

"If we're alone, we won't be talking," she replied, seeing right through that little ploy. He smiled at her, oozing smooth confidence and lethal charm and the Darwinian ability to fight until he was the only one standing. All things that drew her to him in the first place. In a desperate defensive maneuver, she tried to conjure up Mark Anthony. Failed.

Mark Anthony was a dweeb.

"We could talk after," he teased.

"Sean, I can't do this. I'm around you, and I can't think."

He grinned and took a step closer, narrowing the distance to nothing, which only made it more difficult to think. "We call that love. There is nothing that can't be solved with earnest negotiations."

"You can't fix this, Sean," she said tiredly. Last night she'd gotten zero sleep, waking up every hour on the hour. At 3:00 a.m., she was wide awake, listening to him saying he loved her on her voice mail once again.

"Maybe I can't fix this, but I bet there's a solution we haven't considered. I think we should analyze all sides in great detail," he said, pressing a kiss against her neck, and the nonthinking was back in full force.

Cleo's first instinct was to rub shamelessly against him, but honestly, it wasn't necessary. He knew. It was there in the gleaming dark eyes that were full of great details—excellent great details.

"Come with me, Cleo. Take a vacation. A weekend. My trial is over on Wednesday, so this weekend would be perfect. We leave on Friday night, after you're off, and come back on Sunday. We can be back early."

"I can't leave my mother alone." She was surprised he'd even bring it up.

"Daniel and Catherine will be here, as will your uncle. I've already cleared it," he explained, completely prepared, and she wondered how he could do this. Lead her down the path of temptation, setting out the perfect bait in front of her nose.

A weekend with Sean. Not long enough to feel guilty, yet more than thirty minutes in a subway station. More than three forbidden hours in a twin bed. More than anything she'd ever wanted in her life.

Immediately, her self-protective impulses kicked in. Anytime that something seemed too good to be true...

"She can wander," she reminded him.

"I know," he reminded her.

"And sometimes she hides the silverware."

"Sometimes Daniel hides the cash. They're really more alike than you know."

"And if she doesn't like someone, she won't eat."

"So does that mean your mother likes me?"

"God help her, but probably, yes." The more he talked, the more feasible it sounded. Almost…sensible. Yet Cleo was worried that that was only because the denial was back. Possibly because his cologne was seducing her nose, his hands were hot on her hips, his mouth tickled her neck, whispering so many promises, and she could feel him pressing thick and urgent between her legs, conveying so many promises there as well.

"We'll go to Vermont. It'll be like Switzerland. Neutral, with a cold climate. No opposing sides. No battles. We'll talk," he said, his mouth trailing down even lower, delving into the rise of her breast.

"I thought the purpose of this was to talk," she told him, her voice weak.

He lifted his head, met her eyes, trapping her there. "You're right. I want to talk. Do you know how many things I don't know about you? I don't know if you snore or talk in your sleep or what you like for breakfast. I don't know your favorite color or if you're a chocolate girl or a vanilla girl or when your birthday is or if you prefer sushi or Thai or Korean or if you read your horoscope on a daily basis. I want to know these things, Cleo. Mostly I want to know why you told me you love me in a voice mail rather than in person."

She didn't want to answer this question, oh, she knew it was a bad idea, but she wouldn't lie to him, either. "Because if I told you in person, I wouldn't walk away."

He rested his forehead against hers. "Oh, Cleo. What are you doing?"

"I don't know," she whispered.

"Come with me. You owe me. Think of all the pain and suffering you have caused. There are damages there. Compensatory damages that you owe me, Cleo." He put her hand over his heart. "Do you feel the heel marks there, Cleo? Stiletto heels where you have trampled all over my weak and worthless organ. And this," he said, moving her hand down lower to cover his erection. "Calcified from lack of use. An unintended side effect of Cleo-love-gone-wrong." He was making a joke, but there was no humor in his eyes, only pain. He was miserable without her, stressed and overworked with her. Why had she ever thought this could work?

"You owe me this, Cleo," he continued, mercilessly playing on her guilt. "Two days. That's all I'm asking. You want me to beg, Cleo, and I'll do it. I don't have a choice."

In the end, she didn't have a choice, either. "We'll leave on Friday," she told him, and his mouth fell on hers, hungry and hot, and the fire was there, burning like it always was.

"Sean, this can't last. It'll wear out."

"Do you think that, Cleo? I don't. This is me. Fast, furious and a thousand degrees. This is you, too. Standard operating procedure. Don't you know that? We'll both get worn, but we won't be worn out. At least not for me. You're it."

God help them both. She smiled at him, worried, and was more than slightly uncertain, but there was no more denying the truth. "You're it for me, too."

VERMONT WAS PERFECT. Cleo felt guilty that she loved it so much. She thought she should be miserable, so she frowned, but then she would look at Sean and start smiling again, as if everything was fine, which only made her feel guilty again.

She had stayed up all night on Thursday to get ready for this trip. She had typed up instructions and phone numbers, an entire emergency plan and went over everything in detail with Daniel and Catherine. She baked her mother sugar cookies and tried to explain to her that she was going away, but her mother didn't know her any more, but Cleo explained anyway, just in case maybe, deep inside, her mother knew.

By the time they got to Vermont it was night. The roads were black and deserted. And outside a quaint town was the A-frame ski chalet that Sean said belonged to one of the partners at the firm. And man, those partners had style.

It was crafted in wood with big fluffy rugs and a stone fireplace with logs stacked neatly to the side. When you looked out the big bay window, the moon cast its light on the snow-covered mountains. It truly was perfect. So quiet, so peaceful.

Sean made them a late dinner. Pasta, salad, bread and wine. While Cleo watched him work in the kitchen, she could feel herself getting accustomed to this. She could feel her hard shell turning soft, and she kept trying to remember that she shouldn't get used to this because, once she got back home, it was back to the tensions of the real world. However, there was a voice in the corner of her mind that kept whispering, telling her that things could be different.

After dinner, they sat in front of the fire, and Sean didn't seem to mind that she didn't want to talk. She wasn't sure she was ready to talk, so she sat there next to him, not quite touching, but close enough to be there with him, and he understood. She was used to sex, used to fighting, used to work, but this quiet intimacy was new and unnerving. The fire was almost hypnotic, the red and orange sparks popping, and the wine made her so warm, so happy. Or maybe that was Sean.

Cleo laid down on the fluffy rug, and pillowed her head on her hands, and he started to rub her shoulders, finding the exact perfect spot that made her purr, and this time she was not going to feel guilty. Cleo was going to have her moment, and she was going to enjoy it. She was going to enjoy him.

Her lips curved up in a smile and her eyes drifted shut. Cleo fell asleep.

CLEO CAME AWAKE, her hands unclenching from the pillow, her feet automatically reaching for the floor. She had forgotten to lock the door and she needed to lock the door with the key, because one time she had forgotten and her mother had woken before her and the outcome was not fun. When her bare toes didn't touch hardwood floors but instead sank into soft carpet, she realized her mistake.

Sean reached for her and pulled her back down into bed, back into his arms. At some point, he had moved her there. She was still wearing the heavy wool sweater and jeans she'd worn earlier, but he was in his shorts, his chest warm and broad. Quickly, she stripped out of her clothes. After a few sex experiences with tangled clothes or tiny beds, this time she wanted to hold him amidst the tangle of bare flesh. Immediately she knew the difference, felt the difference. Coyly, because she could, she curled one of her legs over his, and sucked in her breath. His skin was like a blast of heat. In a place where the outside was so cold, in here, lying next to him, was intoxicatingly warm. His thighs were a hard mass of thick muscle, and in between his thighs…

Cleo smiled.

Somebody wasn't asleep.

He was waiting for her. He'd always been waiting for her. Gently, she touched his lips with hers and kissed him. Sean O'Sullivan had taught her the humbling power of a kiss, the foolish need to lay herself down in front of another person and invite them to see her. Full, frontal exposure to all her vulnerabilities, all her weaknesses, all her flaws. In Cleo's world, vulnerabilities were carefully masked and hidden because there was always someone there waiting to take advantage, but Sean never would. She knew that now. Maybe she'd always known that.

She opened her mouth against his, tasting him, feeling the power coiled inside him. It was there under her hand, waiting for her. Her palm slid over his chest, the bristling whorls of hair, the sharpness of a male nipple under the pads of her fingers. All that power, and he was letting her control it, control him. Her hands slid lower, burrowed into his shorts, and she heard his breathing stop.

In an instant, the shorts were gone, and Cleo was splayed underneath him.

"I've waited for forever to seduce you," he whispered. His hand skimmed over her, the delicate spot at the base of neck, the softness of her breast, the fragile shield covering her heart, and she wasn't afraid. Not anymore. She was done fighting this. She couldn't.

His mouth traced the line of her body, whispering words to her—beautiful, golden words that no man had ever whispered before. His lips feasted on her, following the rise of her breasts, first one, then the other. She'd been feared, respected and hated, but never adored. Her heartbeat stuttered in fear, then slowly, steadily, he erased the fear because this was Sean, master of the impossible. Her body melted, the ice turning first warm, then hot, then to liquid fire. He pushed the covers aside, and she stretched in the moonlight, drawing his eyes.

He knelt over her, her fingers tracing the lines of his broad shoulders, testing the strength of those killer thighs, needing to touch, needing to learn. For endless moments, they explored each other. He found the freckle on the inside of her thigh, ripping a groan from her mouth. She drew her nails down the line of his back, his buttocks, and he shuddered against her. Cleo had chased the two-minute orgasm her entire adult life, but this was new. It was as if they had *all the time in the world....*

ALL THE TIME IN THE world. Sean had told himself that tonight was about going slow, savoring her, pleasuring her, discovering her, but every time he looked at her, every time those amber eyes peered up at him, sleepy and passion filled, he forget his good intentions.

She had the body of a siren, snow-white skin that reflected the moon. High breasts with nipples like rosebuds. Her hair spread over her shoulders, over the pillows, and it was a picture that he would take to the grave. Her legs were long and lean, a constellation of freckles dotting her thighs. And in between her thighs, was the patch of fire that called to him, lured him to its heat.

"Take me," she said softly, the words going to his head, igniting the need once again. He'd never needed a woman before, but then again, he'd never met Cleo before. He parted her legs because he couldn't wait. Even with all the time in the world, he couldn't wait. He slid inside her, feeling Cleo surround him, feeling Cleo love him.

Her hips shifted and he thrust, and this wasn't a fight, wasn't a battle. Her body stretched, moved, accommodating. Pax. Slowly he moved—push, retreat, back and again—as if the world had stopped, as if time had stopped.

Sean rose on his arms, and she watched him in the moonlight, possessively. He'd never seen that from her. Possession. His eyes met hers, locked there, and they didn't need words.

His hips moved faster, and Cleo locked her legs around his hips and met him, her back arching. Her mouth fell open, the coming orgasm showing there in her eyes, and he wasn't gentle anymore, but neither was she. He lifted her hips, watching where there bodies were joined, and sweat bloomed on her bare flesh, one drop trickling down her breast, gliding along the smooth skin, tempting him.

"Cleo," he taunted her, because it was a matter of pride. "You're mine, Cleo. Did you know that?"

She leaned back, arched before him like a feast and smiled. "No."

He pounded, driving deeper, harder, and he felt the fire burning inside him, scorching him. That was her. "Yes," he told her. "Yes, yes, yes."

Almost. She was close, so close, but she narrowed her eyes, determined not to give in. Her nails raked down his back, down deep into the muscles there and dug. Hard.

He grabbed her hands, and pulled them over her head until she was helpless. And he didn't stop. His body didn't stop moving for a moment, and all she could do was lie there, taking him in. Her legs kicked up, but he moved his thigh, locking her there.

He leaned down, put his mouth on her breast and sucked. Hard.

Cleo nearly screamed. She would have, except for the fact that she knew he was waiting for it, anticipating it.

And then, as quickly as the battle had started, it faded, and Sean lowered himself on top of her like a blanket, and his hips slowed, and his face was there, next to hers, so close that she could almost…nip at him, if she desired. And oh yes, she desired, but not that, not to hurt him. He was the most beautiful animal in the world. All predatory strength, all protective warmth and all hers.

Cleo smiled at him, and he smiled back, and she thought it was the most beautiful smile in the world. "Yes," he whispered, playing at her mouth with his teeth, teasing.

"No," she answered, her hips rising to meet him, each thrust moving deeper inside her, going farther and closer to her heart.

"Yes," he whispered, taking her mouth and feeding, his tongue moving with his hips, with her tongue, with her hips. For a long time, endless and quiet, he moved inside her, completely in sync until finally her body froze. He thrust again, higher, deeper, hitting the one muscle inside her that she had protected so carefully. Her heart.

She let herself take the plunge, and afterwards, he gathered her close, her back to his chest, and she could feel the heavy rise and fall.

"You're going to be the death of me, aren't you?" he asked, his mouth hot on her neck.

Cleo closed her eyes, completely at peace with the world. She kissed the hand that protected her so fiercely. "Yes," she breathed.

Finally.

THEY STAYED IN BED the entire day. That hadn't been Cleo's plan, but when he woke up, she started to talk, and two hours later, they were still talking. At first Cleo rambled on about work, telling him the stories that she never had told anyone, not because they were so top secret, but merely because it had been years since she had talked to anyone, and in that time, she had built up things inside her, stories, and apparently today, they decided to all come out.

Sean held her close, listening as she jumped from one topic to another. At first she waited for sex, because she could feel his arousal against her thigh like a brand, but he was waiting, and she wasn't sure why, but the light in his eyes was so soft and so compelling, and she was drowning here, falling into the deep waters far from her safe, comfortable middle ground.

"I shouldn't talk so much," she told him by way of an apology, but he shrugged, and her gaze drifted over his chest, but he still made no moves toward sex, and now she knew he was waiting on purpose.

He asked her all those questions he had told her he wanted to know. They argued over her snoring because she didn't think she did. They argued over the plans for the West Side park, but the fights never went anywhere. There was too much love.

Eventually, she made him talk about his trial, his cases, his family. She truly didn't want to monopolize the conversation, and the sun was starting to come up in the window and made her conscious of time. There were no clocks here, and he'd taken away her phone and her watch and her beeper, but time didn't stop, even when you took away all the tools that helped you tame it.

He didn't say a word about the pro bono stuff, so she asked him about it, and a flush crept into his cheeks, and he still dodged it, but Cleo was excellent at getting what she wanted, and he didn't protest too much.

"Do you ever think about changing specialties?" she asked, because his face was different when he talked about the other cases.

"No. I'm where I'm at for a reason. The system needs lawyers like me."

"What does that mean?" she asked, fascinated to see how his mind worked. The rationalizations, the reasons.

"Most people see things as all good or all bad. A thief, all bad. A victim, all good, but in justice, you have to differentiate the act from the person. A great person can kill and still be guilty. The worst asshole in the world can be mugged and still not deserve it. I try not to judge people, and there aren't many lawyers that don't."

"I think it's very sexy," she told him.

"Being nonjudgmental?"

"Being a lawyer."

He laughed, sweeping a hand down her side, making her shiver. "I think I'm in love."

"I think you're deluded," she told him, partially kidding, partially…not.

"Cleo," he stared, frowning, and it was that ominous tone that got to her, for a little bit longer she wanted this escape.

"I love you," she told him. It was a cheap, diversionary shot, but it worked. He gathered her in his arms exactly how she wanted him to, met her mouth exactly how she had dreamed, and a cheap, diversionary shot had never turned so quickly to heaven.

FOR EVERY MOMENT in heaven, there is an equal and opposite corresponding moment in hell. It was late on Saturday night when even Cleo knew that the time for denial was over.

"You wanted to talk," she began.

"I think we should," he countered. "Have you thought about the future, Cleo? Really thought?"

"At first I didn't. When I started taking care of Mom, the first two years were easy. I thought it was a breeze. If she forgot her keys, that was a bad day back then. I started paying the bills and checked the refrigerator for old food. My uncle took care of the errands and repairs around the apartment, but I was sure we could take care of everything. The next three years, she got worse, and Elliott got older and less able to do stuff, and it fell more and more on me. In all that time, she never got aggressive or moody or ill-tempered. I think I'm the one with those genes, Mother was never like that. Gradually things went downhill, so gradually that I never noticed it. I don't think I can point to one day where I thought, hell, what am I doing? But I'm doing the right thing, Sean. I know it. It's not for everybody. Not everybody is as strong as I am, but I can do this."

He was watching her intently and she sighed. "You think I'm an idiot."

Slowly, he shook his head. "No. Not an idiot. Someone who loves greatly."

He made it sound so much nicer than ludicrous. She touched his hand. "I would do the same for you."

"I thought you were dumping me," he said, looking at her with those sly, lawyer eyes.

"I should. I can't."

"I'm glad."

"Can you not be so—you know, volunteering, and needing-to-help-me-out sort of stuff? It will kill you, Sean. I don't want that."

"It won't kill me, Cleo. I'm a big boy. I can take care of myself."

"I should be the one taking care of you," she muttered. He deserved the proper sort of female. One who was there when he needed her, not vice versa. Of course, if he did have that proper sort of female, Cleo would have to strangle her, so perhaps it was for the best.

He pulled her on top of him, his eyes glittering. "You want to take care of me? Come here, woman. I'm feeling neglected."

Cleo rose up over him and smiled, and soon she made him feel loved. Very, very loved.

14

On Monday, Sean awoke to an empty bed. At first, he thought that she'd been there with him. He could smell her, see the indentation in his pillow, feel her underneath him, and then reality struck.

Alone.

He was going to have to get used to that. But for Cleo he would. She was the one woman in the world that he didn't have to pretend with. She liked the rough words. She liked the sharp teeth, and for a moment Sean distracted himself, which was pretty much her fault, too. Not that their relationship wasn't based on something more than rough sex, it was. Not that the sex was really that rough, although he did have some ideas. *Suggestions,* really. To see if her eyes would light up. He thought they would.

But suggestions wouldn't win points with his boss, only weird looks, and today he was back to the grind, and he needed the focus.

The woman was going to kill him.

Sean wound the tie around his neck, and expertly knotted it.

One last look in the mirror, and he frowned again.

How could she not love that? They would survive. Somehow. They had to because he needed her.

Work was surprisingly busy, considering the upcoming

Thanksgiving week holiday. He brought in truffles for Maureen, made her coffee and called Katy from Legal Aid, trolling for cases. Sad. At ten, Pete called.

"You asked me to call when I heard some news on the West Side Stadium. I heard some news. Hizzoner is speaking today near the Javits Center. You should go, Sean. Listen. Listen very carefully."

The West Side Stadium. Within spitting distance of Gabe's bar. Within parking distance, within condo-building distance, within luxury-box distance. Sean closed his eyes and swore.

MANNY FROM THE speechwriting department, *her* speechwriting department, told Cleo about the mayor's speech. Cleo hadn't been paying attention, she'd been distracted, caught up in other things. For instance, her own personal traumas, and her love life, which was quickly becoming much more satisfying than a daytime soap opera. However, when Manny started to talk about the afternoon's upcoming speech, she began to pay attention. She began to pay *careful* attention.

She called Bobby a name. A nasty, vile name, and Manny looked at her in surprise. "Don't like the speech?"

"Not you. Something else. Gotta go."

She checked in with her secretary. "I'm off to the Javits Center."

"For the speech? Bobby will be happy about the support."

Cleo smiled, exposing sharp, white teeth. "Yes, he will."

He had started by the time she arrived, and she stayed near the back, out of the view of the press. Bobby should have told her, he should have clued her in on his plan. She helped him get to this office. He owed her that much.

The speech was fabulous, visionary, as he laid out his

grand plan for the West Side Stadium, complete with watercolor renderings that made the audience go "ohhhhh." It was everything a mayor running for re-election would want. *Bastard.*

As she stood there, watching, listening, she argued with herself, using logic and reason, because she needed to be smart. If she wasn't smart, she would no longer be Cleo Hollings, Deputy Mayor, she would only be Cleo Hollings, unemployed, and she really, really couldn't afford that now. However, she wasn't going to let Bobby do this to Sean. Bobby didn't care about Sean. He didn't even know Sean. To Bobby, Prime was nothing more than a gnat, a minor annoyance to be handled.

But not if Cleo "handled" him first. After the press left, Cleo made her move.

"Bobby, we should talk about this." She wore her best smile. The one that she knew he liked.

He stood there in the blue Brooks Brothers that matched his eyes, so proud, so mayoral. "There's nothing to talk about. Some of the biggest pockets in this city are backing this project. We got ball teams, cable companies, real estate developers and the transit authority all on board. Do you know how often the planets line up like that?"

Possibly yes, but she could play the voter card. "Nobody wanted this stadium the first time it showed up."

"But this is the new and improved plan," he protested, clearly blinded by the dollar signs in his eyes.

"Politically, you're making a bad mistake. Bad mistake, Bobby. You could lose re-election on this one issue alone."

"The city's smart. They'll trade the traffic for the blue-collar jobs that this will bring in."

"Not that many, and they'll go away when the stadium is built and then all we're stuck with is traffic."

"But I'll be out of office by then."

"Mayor, yes, but you've got plans. Governor, senator. It's political suicide."

"No."

"Bobby," she warned, with a hint of steel in her voice. She didn't use it with him, ever. But he'd heard it before, and he understood. His eyes narrowed.

"Don't fight me on this, Cleo. You won't win, and you know how you hate to lose."

"Bobby—"

"Cleo." She knew that voice. She loved that voice. It was a warning. From Sean.

She turned and looked at him, and he was silently telling her to be quiet. Seriously, Sean should've known better than that. When it came to the people that she loved, Cleo would fight to hell and back and then start all over again. Sean knew that, Bobby didn't.

She turned away. Ignoring him. "Bobby, I'll fight you on this one. I'll fight fair until you start getting ugly, and then I'll load up on the dirt. Don't think I don't remember."

"You know how many Deputy Mayors are in this city? Seven, and you know how many people would kill to be Deputy Mayor? I can think of four hundred qualified candidates off the top of my head."

"Cleo—" That, from Sean.

"Fire me," she taunted. "See if I care. I can sue. Wrongful termination. That stellar performance review last quarter, well, it might bite you in the ass, boss."

"You don't have a case."

"Actually. Technically. *Legally*. She does." That, from Sean.

Bobby McNamara turned, and for the first became aware of Sean. Lawyer. Shark. The man she loved. "Who are you?"

"I'm Miss Hollings legal representation. Sean O'Sullivan. And you should know that everything you said just got recorded."

"That's illegal."

Sean looked around at the open air, the river in the background. "Public venue. No expectation of privacy. Oops. But…let's not talk lawsuits. That's such an ugly word, and I can think of something that will make both of you happy. Now, Your Honor, voters aren't going to be happy about the stadium. You know that, you think that with all that money lining your campaign coffers you don't have to care. However, what if you could get eight million voters on your side? What if you came up with something beneficial to the community, at no cost to the city, and of huge political benefit to you?"

"It doesn't exist. I've worked in civic government for the last fifteen years, and there's always a price tag."

"Yes, there will be, but this one can be sucked up by people who can afford it."

"Sean," started Cleo. She wasn't sure where this was going, but it probably wasn't going to be good.

He held up a hand. "Now think about this carefully before you say anything because this will work. A clinic. The Harlem clinic that you wanted but which just sadly got killed for budgetary reasons. A low-income clinic specializing in pediatric respiratory diseases. The premier pediatric respiratory research facility in the nation. All those sick kids, trying to breathe smog-infested fumes. I could quote statistics that would curl your hair…. But what if the Bobby McNamara Pediatric Respiratory Center opened? What if the medical community banded together to donate time and dollars?"

"And why would they do that?" asked Bobby, his voice dripping with skepticism.

Cleo knew the answer to this one. She started to smile.

"I work for McFadden Burnett. Medical malpractice. I'm the best damned medical malpractice defense lawyer in this city, probably in the nation, but I don't want to brag. Do you know what that means?"

"What?" asked Bobby, who was usually sharper than this.

"All those doctors, all those hospitals, all those medical professionals that I defend zealously within the constricts of the law…they owe me, Bobby. Big time. And today only, I'm willing to work that in your favor. But this offer isn't going to last long because I'm not a patient man. Think about it. Gridlock, long lines of traffic clogging the West Side Highway on Game Day Sunday, or healing poor, sick kids? How's that going to play on the six o'clock news? Do you know how many times Giuliani made the cover of *Time?* Seven. Bloomberg? Four. McNamara? Well, gee."

"Why should I believe you?"

This time Cleo spoke up. "Ask anybody in this town about Sean O'Sullivan and see what sort of answers you'll get. You'll get convinced real fast, Bobby."

Sean nodded modestly. "Do your homework, mayor. If I were in your shoes, I would. I'll give you a week."

THE MAYOR LEFT and Cleo dawdled nearby, waiting until most of the remaining people had left for newer, more exciting ventures. Sean watched her closely, feeling better than he'd felt in days, weeks, years. Yeah, she loved him.

"You think you can deliver on all that?" she asked him, still doubting his ability to work miracles. Someday she was going to believe in him as much as he believed in her.

"Oh yeah. Trust me. I have a long memory and take

copious notes, and if anybody doubts it, I'll threaten to switch sides. Nobody would ever, ever want me working for the plaintiffs. *Ever.*"

"Why don't you work for the plaintiffs?" she asked. He suspected she thought there was more good in him than there really was.

"It all evens out. Everybody wants to think the doctors and the hospitals and pharma are bad people. Until they heal them or cure them or in general save someone's life. I defend the other side, too, so don't worry. I haven't sold my soul. Not yet." He stuffed his hands in his pockets, trying not to grin. Possibly failing. "So, that's a pretty gutsy thing you did. Nearly got yourself fired. Gutsy and foolish, too."

"I wasn't worried."

"Oh?"

She shook her head. "Because you'd be there, wouldn't you?"

And Cleo was getting smart. "Yeah."

"See, with you at my back, I don't worry as much. It was a very freeing revelation."

Time to bait the hook, sway the jury. "I thought you were tougher than that. I thought you were handling everything on your own."

She looked at him and sighed. "I don't want to handle it on my own, Sean. I'm tired of being a cold, bitter person at thirty-one. I want to be happy. You make me happy. It's a little frightening, and I don't want to psychoanalyze it, but you do. You make me feel safe, happy and loved. And I can get used to that."

This time he grinned, and he didn't care that she saw. "That's my girl. I knew you'd come around."

"You and your ego."

"Force of will. Very powerful stuff."

The light fell from her eyes, and his grin fell as well. "Sean, what am I going to do?"

"You're asking my advice? Hell froze, didn't it? Little piggies flitting across the sky?" He really wanted that light back, and he wasn't sure he could put it back.

Her mouth tightened. "Don't make me regret my decision."

He took her hand in his. "I won't ever let you regret your decision. Trust me. While I've been awake, lying in my pitifully lonely bed, I've been thinking, and not completely about sex. You do have options. You want to care for your mom at home, that's okay. What would you think about a town house in the city for all of us? Somewhere with a big garden on the ground floor for her to walk in, and plenty of room for live-in staff and several bedrooms."

"I'm Deputy Mayor, not CEO of Goldman-Sachs. I can't afford that." Her eyes were so skeptical. Oh, ye of little faith.

"I can. It's really obscene what they pay lawyers in this town. Next year, I'll make partner. Then the money will truly be shocking, you might have to sit down. Now it is true that, with that sort of real estate, it is pricey. You might have to forgo that summer in Europe, but we'll scrape by."

There. The light was back. He'd put it there. "You don't know what you're getting into, Sean."

Sean pulled her closer, watching her eyes flare. Yeah, he'd put that there, too. She was perfect for him, he was perfect for her, and once again, Cleo was a little slow catching up. They'd have to work on that. "I do. I know exactly what I'm getting into, Cleo. We'll work this out. Your mother needs you right now and you need to take care of her, and don't worry about me."

"What are you getting out of this?" she asked suspiciously, but she didn't realize that he was getting the best end of the deal. He was getting her.

"I get to take advantage of your tender sensibilities whenever I have the chance. It's a very fair settlement offer, you should take it."

Her hips shifted against him, subtle, wicked. *Cruel.* God, he loved her. "I don't have tender sensibilities."

"You want to bet?"

"Yes, yes, I do," she said, one long, long leg impudently sliding in between his thighs.

Sean kissed her then. Long and hard. "You are going to be the death of me. I know it."

ON THE THIRD THURSDAY in November, all eyes turned to the red awning on Thirty-forth Street. Macy's. Home of the Macy's Thanksgiving Day parade. It wasn't every day that Sean got to sit under the awning, but today he was a guest. A guest of the Deputy Mayor, her mother and her uncle.

The grand marshal was about to kick it off—Sean didn't really care who it was—he was there for one person only. The mouthy redhead with amber eyes and a world-class glare that never failed to stir his cock.

Sad. Very sad.

But today wouldn't be so bad. In fact, it was going to be kind of fun. He could see her coming. Truthfully, he could spot her from a mile away, all his senses honing in. She walked up to see her mother, hugged her, and he was happy to see that the circles were starting to disappear from her eyes. Things weren't easy. They would never be easy with Cleo, but he had no choice. She was his other half.

"Mom?" she asked warily and Rachel Hollings

looked at her daughter with the remarkable love that seemed to run in the Hollings family.

Her mother turned to her. "Look at you in your amber suit. I told you that it matches your eyes. I don't think New York ever had a more beautiful Deputy Mayor."

"Thank you, Mom," she said, and Sean watched as she blushed like a girl.

The Wicked Witch of Murray Street, not likely.

"You've got everything under control?" she asked him, still doubting his abilities.

"We're fine, Cleo. There're eight cops here. Not going anywhere. Do your whole car-riding, waving thing and we'll have a good time watching. I'll be especially happy to watch."

Cleo looked around and worried her lip. "Okay, you're right. Everything is fine," she said, starting to make her escape.

He held out his hand. "Pay up."

"Sean!" she said in an outraged whisper.

He sighed. With a low voice, he asked, "You didn't think I'd let this slide, did you?"

She looked so the picture of wronged innocence. He knew Cleo would do great on the stand. "You cheated," she accused.

Sean shook his head. "Did not. There were no rules. There is no cheating when there are no rules. Next time, I'll draft a contract if it'll make you happy. Right now, pay up."

She looked around, sidled close, and yeah, he had her. Discreetly she stuck a pair of black silk panties in his pocket. Oh, damn, that felt good.

However, Sean was not easily duped. Since he'd known her, he'd learned what she was capable of, not all of it pretty, but yes, it was fun. He slid a hand over her back, over her waist, momentarily dipping lower and fondling her ass, and yep, nothing there. He exhaled a glorious sigh of victory.

She glared. "You're *so* going to pay for this."

He brought her close. "Keep your thighs together when you're riding on that seat and no one will ever know." He grinned. "Except for me."

"You think you're so smart, don't you," she said, her hand drifting down, flirting lower, and he sucked in a breath, since she knew his weak spots. That was definitely one.

"I got you this time," she whispered, and caught his hands behind his back, bracketing them together. Sean wasn't focusing; he was caught up in the devil in her eyes.

Snap.

That wasn't warm flesh. That was cool steel. Sean tried to pull his hands apart, but he knew instantly. Handcuffs.

"Cleo," he warned…

"Sean," she whispered, brushing up against him, teasing and smiling, like the bloodthirsty woman she was.

Casually, she looked at the surrounding officers and waved, as if she didn't know that she owned his heart. "Police force. They work for me, Sean. You really don't know who you're messing with."

Then she walked off, leaving him seething in frustration, leering at her ass, and he knew exactly what was underneath her skirt, and his hands fisted, but the cuffs hurt. That *hurt.* She didn't care that this was killing him. She didn't care that anyone might see what had to be his most painful erection ever, *ever,* pushing out his pants. Oh, no, she was leaving him there, with her mother and uncle, handcuffed, surrounded by eight of New York City's finest.

All of them snickering.

"Cleo!" he yelled.

She turned and waved, probably the same one she was going to use when she was sitting up on that seat, long legs, sleek thighs, leading to…

Nope. Sean, don't be stupid. He needed to think about something else. Like revenge for instance.

When he got her alone, she was going to pay. *She was going to pay.*

Sensing his misery, Rachel Hollings turned to Sean and smiled. "You're going to have to watch your step, young man," she said, her eyes bright and aware. "You see, that's my daughter."

Epilogue

FOR THOSE WHO'D WORRIED, Tessa and Gabe were married the following year two weeks after Sean and Cleo because Sean swore he would not be last.

After their marriage, Tessa and Gabe elected not to have children because Tessa was worried that if they had a daughter she would follow in her mother's foolhardy footsteps and get a moronic tattoo, and Tessa felt like it was an issue. Instead, they had nine cats, most of them fat, and Tessa went on to become one of Corcoran's best-selling real estate agents. Gabe, being Gabe, didn't mind.

Catherine and Daniel had three children: two girls, Amanda and Michelle, and one boy, Joshua. Both girls took up accounting while Josh was the artist. When he was sixteen, his mother told him that if he painted nudes it would cause blindness at an early age. He didn't believe her (rightly so), and went on to become a world-famous artist, whose paintings were sold at the Montefiore Auction House. His mother (after he reached the age of twenty-one) was very proud.

And then there was Cleo and Sean.

New York City's mayor, Bobby McNamara, went on to win his next term in a tight election due to the withdrawal of the high-dollar real estate vote. It took some time for Cleo to untangle all the mayor's bureaucratic nooses around Gabe's bar, and in the process, she discovered a half dozen other businesses caught up in the West Side development scheme, and of course, she fixed those, too. The Bobby McNamara-Rachel Hollings Respiratory Research Clinic opened, though sadly, Rachel Hollings was not alive to appreciate the building's dedication, but Cleo thought her mother knew.

Cleo continued to serve during the second term of the McNamara administration, and then ran for mayor herself and won. Although there were rumors that Sean O'Sullivan had bought up some of the vote, the allegations were never proven, and actually, technically, *legally,* with the large turnout from both the medical community and the New York City bar association—all dedicated voters—it really wasn't necessary anyway.

They went on to have two children: a daughter, Rachel, and a son, Peter.

At the age of six, Rachel O'Sullivan announced to her family that she was going to be President of the United States. Forty years later, on a cold January day, Rachel O'Sullivan was sworn in and moved in to the White House. Both mother and father stood by to watch, and Cleo nearly cried, but she insisted that it was only the wind.

Their son Peter O'Sullivan was not nearly so ambitious. At the Christmas of his tenth year, he announced his dream. He wanted to run a bar.

The entire family applauded.

* * * * *

Heidi isn't the kind of woman to leave her life to chance. Her plan? To marry her perfect boyfriend Jesse and have several perfect children. Unfortunately, the only perfect thing in her life lately is the sizzling hot attraction she shares with Jesse's best friend Kyle...

Turn the page for a sneak preview of

Reckless
by Tori Carrington,

*available from Mills & Boon® Blaze®
in November 2009*

Reckless
by
Tori Carrington

HOT BREATH created a steamy dampness on her neck, challenging the summer heat for dominance… Her nipples awakened to tingling life under the attention of his roaming hands… She tightened her thighs, trapping his hips, a moan building in her throat…

Heidi Joblowski arched her back against the cool sheets and slid her hands down to cup Jesse's bottom, holding him close.

Oh, yes…

He instantly stiffened against her, his body quaking.

Oh, no.

Not again. Not yet.

Heidi bit her bottom lip, praying that this wasn't it. That Jesse wasn't finished.

He collapsed against her.

The moan turned into a groan.

"Mmm," he hummed, kissing her neck several times and then kissing her mouth. "That was good. You were good."

Apparently she was too good. He'd reached climax before she was even halfway up the ladder, leaving her hanging from the rungs with no hope of his helping her over. Because she knew that no matter what she said, what she did, he was done.

And she wasn't even close.

"What?" he said when she kissed him back with moderate enthusiasm. "Oh, no. Did I do it again?"

Heidi took a deep breath, trying to unwind her coiled muscles. "When I said 'quickie,' I didn't mean it in a literal sense. I meant 'no foreplay necessary.' But an orgasm would have been nice."

He chuckled into her hair. "I'm sorry, Heidi."

She stretched her neck, figuring she could see to herself in the shower. After all, it was three o'clock on a busy Saturday afternoon in June and she certainly hadn't expected more. Had hoped for more, especially since they'd spoken several times lately about Jesse's habit of not waiting for her before diving over the orgasmic edge.

Of course, all it usually took for Jesse was a gentle blow in his ear and a squeeze of her thighs and he was a goner.

Therein lay the problem.

"It's the place, I think," he said, smoothing her hair back from her face. "It's strange having sex in Professor Tanner's place."

"It's not his place, it's mine. At least for the summer while I'm renting it from him."

Well, she was actually house-sitting, as well. Watering Tanner's plants, taking care of his garden, forwarding his mail to him while he was in Belgium for the next couple of months. A perfect set-up, really. She got the type of privacy with Jesse that she wanted and that they couldn't have at the apartment he shared with two friends, and all she had to do was take care of the house as if it were her own. Perfect.

Only it wasn't working as well as she'd hoped.

Jesse turned on his dazzling megawatt grin. "Do you want to try again?"

Heidi quickly reached for another condom on the nightstand.

A knock at the front door thwarted her intentions.

Jesse kissed her. "I'll make it up to you, Hi. I promise."

She languidly snaked her arms around his neck and tunneled her fingers into his thick, dark hair. "At this rate, you'll owe me well into the next century," she whispered.

His chuckle made her smile. "So be it." He kissed her deeply again before pushing off to jump into his jeans sans underwear. "I can come up with worse debts."

So could she.

Heidi propped herself up on her elbows, watching Jesse Gilbred's fine male form as he got dressed. His tousled hair dipped low over his brow. His slender, whipcord-taut muscles moved and rippled with his actions. His green eyes twinkled at her mischievously.

It was a sight of which she'd never tire. She'd met Jesse when they'd been little more than kids in high school and had remained smitten with him ever since. He'd been the captain of the football team, she'd been the quiet, studious girl from the wrong side of the tracks. Even when he'd left Fantasy, Michigan, to attend college in the east, they'd maintained a long-distance relationship, with Jesse returning at least one weekend a month to see her. It had been a long two years, but when he'd graduated and come home for good to work in a managerial capacity at his father's construction company, she'd been there for him, just as she had for the past eight years.

He had been her first. And she intended that he be

her last. He was the one she'd built all of her plans around. Well, all but the little detail they encountered every now and again, as they had just now. But they could definitely work on that.

He left the room and Heidi pulled a pillow over her head and gave a muffled moan.

"Hey, how's it hanging, man?" she heard Jesse's voice as he greeted their visitor.

She shifted the pillow to peek at the bedroom door he'd left wide open.

Jesse's best friend entered her line of vision, all blond hair and dark tan. He stared at her, apparently as startled as she was at being caught in this situation.

"Jesse!" she called, yanking the sheet up to her chin and then catapulting off the bed so she could close the door.

Heidi leaned against the wood for long moments, listening to Jesse's laugh and Kyle's awkward apologies.

So much for seeing to her own needs. Whatever lingering desire she felt had been chased away by another man's scorching gaze.

She made out Jesse's words through the wood, "No need to apologize. If a guy can't trust his best friend, who can he trust?"

Heidi gave an eye roll and dropped the sheet, stepping over it on her way to the connecting bath.

NAKED as the day she was born.

The ridiculous saying came to Kyle Trapper's mind as he raked his hand through his hair, staring at his friend as if he'd lost a baseball or two on the way to the game.

Kyle had yet to move from where he stood in the middle of the small, well-appointed living room. His gaze wandered back toward the closed bedroom door of its own volition, as if hoping to catch another forbidden glimpse of Heidi's decadent white flesh. He didn't care which part. Whether it was her pert, rose-kissed breasts, her flat, toned stomach, or the trimmed triangle of hair that seemed to point toward the V of her thighs like an erotic arrow.

His friend sat on an armchair pulling on socks and athletic shoes, oblivious to his thoughts. And it was a good thing. If their roles had been reversed, he'd have punched his friend.

"Hell, Jesse, do you let everyone see your girlfriend naked?"

Jesse got up and smacked him on the back. "Only my closest friends."

Kyle was not amused.

"What's your problem? You'd think you'd never seen a woman without her clothes on."

"Never that woman."

Never Jesse's girl.

Jesse grabbed a T-shirt that was hanging on the back of the chair. "How'd you know I was here, anyway?"

Kyle hadn't known. In fact, he hadn't come here for his friend at all. He'd come to talk to Heidi.

He cleared his throat. "Where else would you be?"

His response must have come out gruffer than he'd intended because Jesse paused. "Hey, you never have told me what your problem is with Heidi, but she's one of the most open women I've ever met." He shrugged as he pulled the shirt over his head. "She won't care that you've seen her naked."

"Right. That's why she turned ten shades of red and

slammed the door." Kyle rubbed the back of his neck. "And why do you think I have a problem with her?"

Jesse pulled the T-shirt down, revealing the name of a local tavern. "She thinks you don't like her."

That surprised him. At the same time it was cause for relief. If either Jesse or Heidi had a clue about how he really felt…well, he didn't think he'd be standing in her rental house right now, about to leave with her boyfriend to play softball.

In fact, he'd probably be run out of the small town on a rail, back to a life that had never held much for him by way of a future.

If you had asked him seven years ago where he'd be now, he would never have guessed south-east Michigan, working as an architect. But that would have been before Jesse was assigned as his roommate at Boston University and his life had changed forever…for the better. So much so that he hadn't hesitated when his friend had invited him to come to Fantasy eight months ago and put his architectural talents to good use by working in cooperation with Gilbred Builders. So he'd shut the doors to his own start-up company in Boston and moved to the Midwest.

He'd like to say it had been smooth sailing ever since. But he wasn't much into lying, particularly to himself. Until he'd moved to Fantasy, he'd only spoken to Heidi when she called and Jesse wasn't home—calls he'd enjoyed more than he should have. What he hadn't anticipated was that coming to Fantasy would amplify his lust for a woman he could never have.

If he'd needed a reminder, he'd just gotten it by way

of his uncomfortable physical reaction to a mere glimpse of her full-frontal nudity.

And what of his strategy to combat his unwanted emotions by asking her to help him plan a surprise birthday party for Jesse? The idea being that the more time he forced himself to spend around her, the better he'd be able to battle against his attraction to her? Was he kidding himself by thinking that familiarity would erase whatever mysterious factors drew him to her?

But after eight months of careful avoidance and awkward silences whenever their paths crossed, and nights filled with countless cold showers, Kyle knew he had to do something to defuse a situation that was only getting worse instead of better.

"Anyway, we all know you're gay," Jesse said, lightly hitting him in the arm.

"What?"

"You heard me. I haven't seen you date a single woman since you've come to Fantasy. Back in Boston you were with a girl nearly every night of the week. I figured you'd switched sides and were batting lefty."

Now that was a new one. But, hey, so long as it kept his best friend from learning the truth, let him think what he would.

"I'm joking, man."

Kyle stared at him, realizing that Jesse had expected something else from him. A denial maybe. Or perhaps a mock physical assault.

He made like he was going to slug him.

Jesse laughed and good-naturedly dodged the hit as he grabbed his ball cap. "Come on. We can get in some practice on the field before anyone else gets there."

Jesse opened the front door and walked out. Kyle stood staring at the closed bedroom door for a long moment, feeling as if he owed Heidi an apology. He heard the spray of the shower and swallowed thickly, the sound of the water combining with the memory of her sleekly naked body to create an image he really didn't need.

The blare of a truck horn sounded from the driveway.

Kyle gave the door one last glance and then reluctantly turned away. If he knew what was best for him, he'd keep on going until he was back in Boston and well away from a temptation that had the potential to destroy all the good he'd finally found in life.

© Lori and Tony Karayianni 2008